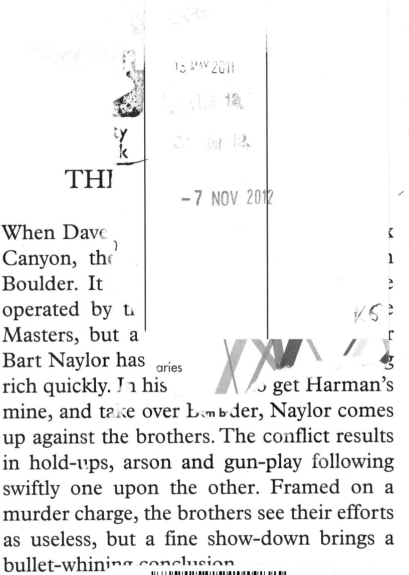

THI

When Dave
Canyon, the
Boulder. It
operated by t
Masters, but a
Bart Naylor has   aries
rich quickly. In his   get Harman's
mine, and take over Boulder, Naylor comes
up against the brothers. The conflict results
in hold-ups, arson and gun-play following
swiftly one upon the other. Framed on a
murder charge, the brothers see their efforts
as useless, but a fine show-down brings a
bullet-whining conclusion

THE STAGE RIDERS

by

Floyd Rogers

Dales Large Print Books
Long Preston, North Yorkshire,
BD23 4ND, England.

British Library Cataloguing in Publication Data.

Rogers, Floyd
    The stage riders.

    A catalogue record of this book is
    available from the British Library

    ISBN   978-1-84262-699-3 pbk

First published in Great Britain in 1967 by Robert Hale Ltd.

Copyright © 1967 Floyd Rogers

Cover illustration © Gordon Crabb by arrangement with
Alison Eldred

The moral right of the author has been asserted

Published in Large Print 2010 by arrangement with
Mr W. D. Spence

Dales Large Print is an imprint of Library Magna Books Ltd.

Printed and bound in Great Britain by
T.J. (International) Ltd., Cornwall, PL28 8RW

1

Clance Masters handled the reins of his team of six firmly but gently in his gloved hands bringing the bouncing stagecoach to a steady speed as he neared Boulder. The tall, fair-haired, young driver wore a worried frown and there was a thoughtful, troubled look in his steel-blue eyes as he turned over in his mind the approach he would make to his older brother, Jed.

Clance could see no future in the stage-coach business. They must be running at a loss almost every trip. This drive certainly would not pay for itself; one passenger from Denver. Clance could not blame anybody; and who would want to come to Boulder, a small place which barely existed, boasted one store, one saloon, one hotel of a sort, about fifty people and not even a sheriff? Clance wanted to sell up for what they could get and leave for some brighter prospects, but as yet he had not brought up the matter with Jed. He knew there was sentimentality attached to the stage-hire. Their father had

7

started the line, had the exclusive rights to this run from the Colorado territorial legislature and had great hopes for its development. His dreams had not materialised and it had passed to Jed and Clance when he had died almost two years ago.

Clance began to slow the horses as they hit the main street. There were a few people on the sidewalks and when they saw the stage some of them started for the office situated half-way along the street opposite the *Golden Nugget Saloon*. The arrival of the stage always brought a group of sightseers, curious to find out who was coming to Boulder. Clance grinned wryly to himself; once again they would be disappointed, only one passenger would alight from the stage.

As he started to pull on the reins and use his right foot on the brake handle, Clance saw his brother step from their office. He knew Jed would be disappointed too, for he realised that Jed was concerned about their financial situation, but, being like their father, Jed always hoped that something would turn up.

The stage rolled to a halt in front of the office. Clance tied the reins round the iron foot rail and climbed down to greet his brown-faced, square-jawed brother. There was a hopeful look in Jed's deep-set, brown eyes as he greeted his brother.

'Good trip, Clance?' he asked.

'Sure, quiet as usual, but only one passenger,' replied Clance turning to open the door of the stagecoach.

The man who climbed stiffly out of the coach was about forty. He was beginning to thicken around the middle and the neck, and his large oval face was heavy jowled. His clothes were shabby and his only possessions were rolled in a cape. He glanced around the small gathering of people who began to turn away and go about their interrupted business, disappointed that there was no one more interesting on the coach.

'Half-hour's break,' Clance informed the new-comer. 'Then I'll take you on to Blackfoot Canyon.'

The stranger nodded and crossed the street towards the *Golden Nugget*.

Jed watched him for a moment. 'No fare from that one, I suppose,' he said dejectedly. 'I expect he's hoping to strike it rich in the canyon.'

'Managed to barter for half,' replied Clance.

'We might get it if he doesn't drink it all in there,' mused Jed.

'I've got it,' answered Clance digging deep into his pocket and extracting the money which he handed to Jed.

'Well, that's something,' said Jed. 'Better than the last trip.'

The two brothers walked into the office of the Masters Overland Stage, and, although he did not relish the moment, Clance was not slow to seize the chance to state his opinion.

'Jed, things aren't going to get better,' he said. 'How long are you going to go on kidding yourself?'

Jed looked at his younger brother. He was somewhat surprised that Clance should have raised the subject of their affairs. Clance was never the deep thinking one; he always acted on the spur of the moment and Jed, on more than one occasion, had got him out of an ugly situation created by his own impetuosity. Jed had always regarded it as a passing phase, one that would disappear with the years.

'I'm not kidding myself, Clance,' replied Jed. 'I never have been.'

'You are,' returned Clance, 'or you would have got out long ago.'

Jed smiled. 'Because I didn't throw in the sponge doesn't mean I have been kidding myself. I know that the stageline is in a precarious position. Maybe I've known it longer than you. I knew it before pa died, but he was proud of this stage run, proud it was his and pleased at the independence it gave him.'

'What's the use of independence if you haven't any money?' retorted Clance. 'If we had to employ anyone we'd go bankrupt. There's no future here, Jed. I think we should sell up for what we can get and leave Boulder; it's a town with no future.' Warmed to the discussion Clance blurted out his ideas.

Although Jed was surprised by Clance's sudden exposure of his attitude he had to agree that there was a lot in what his brother said.

'Maybe you're right, Clance, but pa had faith in this part of the country; he always said this would be an important stage-line.'

'I respect pa,' put in Clance, 'but they were all dreams; pa expected Blackfoot Canyon to yield gold, if it had, well that would have made all the difference, but there's no gold up there, Jed.'

'There could be,' came the quick reply.

'And are we to spend all our lives just hoping that someone strikes it rich? I say we should leave here an' get into the cattle trade. Buy some longhorns, use open range, do a bit of mavericking; Jed we could really

11

get into business.'

Jed smiled at his brother's enthusiasm. He made everything seem so easy, but then everything was to a young man of twenty-one. He remembered how six years ago, at the same age, he had made all sorts of plans to put the stage-line on a sound, paying basis. It was only time which proved to him that it was passengers and freight which made a stage-line profitable. If these were not forthcoming in sufficient quantity then the business either just existed or went broke. He soon realised that Masters Overland Stage fell into the former of these categories but there was always the hope that things might take a turn for the better.

'I still have a feeling that pa might be right,' said Jed thoughtfully. 'I know we've given it a good try. I'll tell you what I'll do. I am pleased to see that you have ambitions, so I don't expect you to stay here; I'll buy your share of the stage-line, that should give you a start with your cattle.'

This suggestion took Clance by surprise. He stared at his older brother for a few moments without speaking. This was typical Jed, stubborn, wanting to hang on until the end and yet not expecting anyone else to be at a disadvantage because of his wishes.

'But where will you raise the money?' asked Clance, anxious to hear more of Jed's idea.

'I'll borrow it from the bank; put our whole set-up into their hands as security,' explained Jed.

'But that would make things twice as hard and twice as precarious for you,' said Clance, amazed at Jed's suggestion. 'You'd do that for me?'

'Sure, why not,' replied Jed. 'You want to leave, I want to stay, so that's the only solution.'

'It isn't,' answered Clance firmly. 'The best solution is for me to stay. That way we still operate without anyone holding demands over our heads.'

'But there's no…' started Jed.

'No buts,' cut in Clance. 'If you're willing to make that sort of sacrifice then I should be willing to stay, after all there's plenty of time and when you see that it's no use hanging on here we'll leave together.' He paused and glanced at Jed. 'Besides, I promised pa I'd stick with you whatever you did.'

Jed grinned and slapped his brother on the shoulder. 'I'm pleased,' was all that he said, but Clance sensed the pleasure and satisfaction Jed felt at his decision.

'I'd better hunt out that prospector and get him up to Blackfoot Canyon,' said Clance.

'We'll have one drink, before you leave,' said Jed, 'just to cement our continued partnership.'

Clance grinned and the two men left their office for the *Golden Nugget*.

They were half-way across the dusty, rutted roadway when the pound of a galloping horse brought them to a stop. They turned to see a rider hitting the main street at an earth-shaking gallop.

'That's Dave Harman!' called Jed.

'Sure must be something wrong for that old-timer to hit town at that pace,' commented Clance.

Dust swirled behind the horse; its head tensed against the pull of the reins as Harman brought it to a sliding halt in front of the saloon. Dave stood in his stirrups, let out one great whoop and tossed his battered hat high in the air.

'I've done it! I've done it! It's a real bonanza!' he yelled at the top of his voice.

He was a small man about sixty. His eyes, alert and eager, reflected the excitement which showed on his lined weather-beaten face, the lower half of which was covered by a bushy beard. His clothes, old and worn, were dust-covered from the ride.

Jed and Clance exchanged glances as they hurried to hear Dave's story. Harman was a familiar figure around Boulder. He was a friendly old man who had known their father well and had chosen to go prospecting rather than become a partner in Masters Overland Stage. For seven years now he had prospected in Blackfoot Canyon, his faith in that land as a source of riches matched his friend's faith in his stage-line. He had taken out only a small quantity of gold, sufficient for his bare needs, but he kept on with his search convinced that he would strike it rich one day.

The townsfolk gathered round Dave excitedly as he swung down from his horse. Questions flew at him, primarily concerned with the location of his strike. Dave laughed as he tried to push his way through the crowd.

'I'm not revealing that until I've staked my claim,' he called out to the questioners. 'There's a sample of what I've found,' he added and pulled out of his pocket a nugget which made everyone gasp.

Jed and Clance who were on the edge of the crowd looked at each other.

'Guess we'd better take care of him,' observed Clance.

'Sure had,' grinned Jed. 'This is the chance we've wanted. If this is true our stage-line is made!'

Dave was having difficulty in pushing his way through the excited crowd but when he suddenly yelled, 'The drinks are on me!' he found himself swept on by the pushing, jostling bodies. Jed and Clance shoved their way forward quickly and as they found themselves on either side of Dave, they each grasped him by the arms. He looked up at them both.

'Hi, boys, wish your pa were here,' he grinned.

'He'd be pleased for you,' said Jed.

The crowd poured through the double-doorway and swarmed across the saloon to the long, mahogany counter. Everyone was talking and yelling. It took only a second for those who had not been outside to learn what all the excitement was about and before long it seemed as if the whole town of Boulder was in the *Golden Nugget*. A way to the bar was made for the lucky man and Jed and Clance lifted him up so that he could sit on the counter. Suggestions, offers and advice poured at Dave, who realised that if he took half of them he would soon have no mine at all.

After about twenty minutes the excitement began to wane in its intensity and the crowd began to split up into groups all still discussing the fortune of Dave Harman. Several men had already left the saloon and were on their way to Blackfoot Canyon, the forerunners of a great horde of people who were to come.

When the crowd began to thin from the counter, Dave jumped down. 'Come on, boys, I want you to drive me into Denver to stake my claim.'

'Guess that'll have to be me,' said Jed, as he spotted the heavily built man, whom Clance had brought in by stage, pushing his was towards them.

'I'd sure like to get up to the canyon,' he said somewhat breathlessly as he reached the three men.

'I guess you would,' grinned Clance.

'You take the buggy,' said Jed. 'I'll take Dave in the stage, I reckon I'll be full of passengers on the return trip.'

The four men left the *Golden Nugget* and a few minutes later the Masters brothers were leaving Boulder in opposite directions.

'Wal, Jed, I guess this should make all the

difference to your stage-line,' observed Dave as the coach swayed out of Boulder on the trail to Denver twenty-five miles to the south-east.

'If there's gold in any quantity up there it sure will,' grinned Jed as he put the horses into a steady pace.

'Quantity!' snorted Dave. 'I'll tell you, son, there'll be more gold up there than anyone dreamed of.'

Jed grinned knowing how the old man could exaggerate.

'You can smile,' went on Dave, 'but what I say is true. At the moment only I know where it is, but I'll tell you, Jed, you're an old friend, seen you raised since you were so high.' He paused and chuckled to himself. 'I left Blackfoot Canyon about a month back and headed into Box Canyon, you know it?'

Jed nodded, recalling the narrow canyon which cut into the mountain three-quarters of the way along the wider Blackfoot Canyon. The latter had been a favourite place for prospectors ever since a few grains of gold had been panned out of the stream which flowed through the canyon. There had been rumours and tales of veins of gold but no one had ever come along with definite evidence and no one, so far as Jed knew, had ever prospected in the narrow Box Canyon. Now he began to wonder if Dave had really hit upon the bonanza for which he had always been searching.

'Well, I found it, Jed, a vein the likes of which you've never seen. You saw the nugget back there, well I've a lot more like it. Wouldn't surprise me if that vein doesn't run clean through the mountain, maybe come out somewhere high up on the side of Blackfoot Canyon.'

'That could account for it not being found and it could account for traces of gold in the stream in the Blackfoot,' commented Jed.

'I tell you, son, it'll make your eyes pop.'

'Dave, will you take advice from a young man?' asked Jed, eyeing the older man seriously.

'What's on your mind, son?' asked Dave.

'Just be careful in Denver,' replied Jed. 'When word of this hits the town there'll be all sorts of sharks on to you.'

Dave grunted. 'Let them all come, old Dave Harman has been around, he can deal with any of them.'

Jed said nothing, knowing Dave's occasional weakness for a bottle of whisky and this was one time when Dave might be tempted to celebrate.

2

Denver was a growing town, already an important jumping off point for travellers heading west. It was the last town of any size before the great barrier of the Rocky Mountains was tackled. It was a thriving town out to make money from the emigrants and from the prospectors from the mountains.

The streets were busy when Jed slowed down the stagecoach on the edge of town. No one took much notice of them as they rolled to a halt outside a stage office which was the Masters Overland Stage agency in Denver. Jed smiled to himself when he thought of the reaction of these people had they known why Dave Harman was in Denver.

Jed poked his head round the door of the office.

'Take care of the horses, Wes, I'll be heading back in about an hour,' he called.

The agent looked up in surprise. 'Didn't expect to see your stage back so soon,' he said, pushing himself out of the chair behind the desk.

'Special trip,' replied Jed.

The agent nodded. 'I'll have them ready.'

Jed stepped back on to the sidewalk. 'Come on, Dave, we'll get to the assay office.'

The two men hurried along the sidewalk, Dave's shorter legs taking three paces to Jed's two. Jed could sense the excitement in the older man when they neared the building and he himself would have admitted to the same feeling. They stopped outside the door of the office.

'Well, Dave, here we are' said Jed grinning at the older man who suddenly seemed nervous. Jed reached out and opened the door, bowed in pleasant mockery and said, 'After you, sir.'

Dave chuckled and cuffed Jed on the shoulder as he swept past him, all signs of nervousness gone. As Jed stepped after him he saw two clerks behind the counter, one of whom was discussing the prospects of finding gold in the mountains to the northwest. Jed was inclined to warn Dave to be cautious but he could not deny the old man the pleasure of a moment he must have dreamed about many times.

Dave strode to the desk, pulled a leather pouch from his pocket, unfastened the thong and emptied the contents on to the desk. Twelve gold nuggets, equal in size to that which he had produced in Boulder, fell on to the mahogany counter.

'I want to stake a claim so I can get more like that,' he announced proudly.

The three men stared in amazement at the nuggets, then they looked at the man who had found them, unable to speak. Dave revelled in the moment. He waited, then looked at each of the clerks in turn.

'Wal, aren't you goin' to register my claim?' he demanded.

That broke the spell. The clerks fussed around; books, papers and maps were produced and Dave's claim registered. Jed noticed that the man, who had been in the office when they arrived, waited long enough to hear where the gold had been found then hurried from the building. A few moments later the door was flung open and men hurried in eager to get a look at the nuggets and their owner. When the business of registering his claim was through, Dave turned to Jed.

'Come on, I reckon we've time to celebrate before we head back,' he said.

'Sure thing,' said Jed.

When the two men stepped outside it was

obvious that the news of the find was going around Denver quicker than a prairie fire. Already plans were being made, horses being saddled, equipment made ready; the whole street seemed to be seething with a new excitement and energy. The inspiring word, gold, was on every lip bringing wild dreams to imaginative minds. People poured from saloons, clamoured in the stores, raced from the barbers' shops and tried to buy horses.

Jed was amazed at the speed with which the news had circulated.

'You sure started a rumpus,' he grinned. Then suddenly the significance of the situation struck him. 'Dave, we'll celebrate in the *Gilded Cage,* Bart Naylor's place. I've got to cash in on this fever. See you there.'

Before the old man could reply Jed was hurrying away in the direction of the office of his agent.

A crowd was already swarming around the office and Jed's stagecoach clamouring to be taken to Blackfoot Canyon. The agent and his assistant were having a difficult time controlling the crowd and keeping the stagecoach horses calm. Jed pushed his way roughly through the milling men until he reached the agent in the doorway of the office. A look of relief came over the small man when he saw Jed beside him.

'I'm sure glad to see you,' he said weakly. 'What are we going to do with them all?'

Jed smiled then turned to the crowd. 'All right, all right,' he yelled at the top of his voice. 'I'm the stagecoach owner, jest calm...' his words were lost in the renewed clamour for seats on the coach. Already the prices offered for seats were fourfold his normal price. Jed tried to shout above the noise but it was no good. Realising he must do something drastic in order to be heard he pulled his Colt from its holster and fired a shot into the air. The crash reacted on the crowd and quietness seemed to flow out from the doorway.

'That's better,' shouted Jed. 'I aim to get as many of you as possible and as quickly as I can to Blackfoot Canyon. In order to do that we must have some organization about it. My stagecoach has the exclusive rights to run between here, Boulder and Blackfoot Canyon, so unless you like to get there by other means I'm your man. If you'll queue up and book a passage with my agent here I'll take you for five dollars for the full trip. There'll be two stages leaving in one hour. One will go as far as Boulder and return, the other will take a double load to the canyon and return to

Boulder. Then we'll be running a shuttle service until you're all fixed up.'

As men started to shove and push their way into a queue along the sidewalk Jed turned to his agent. 'Work out a schedule of departure times from here allowing time to change horses on arrival here. Take their names and allocate them a time. Organise this right and I'll pay you a dollar a passenger.'

'Leave it to me, Jed. But what about the second stage?'

'You hold two teams of horses here I'll have a stage for one of them before long; I'm off to buy one now.'

Jed hurried away, crossed the road and a few minutes later was confronting the bank manager with a request for a loan.

'My stage-line is going to boom on this new strike but I've got to expand and expand quick, in fact right now,' explained Jed enthusiastically. There was a certain hesitation on the bank manager's part. Jed knew the objections, this might not be the boom expected and the Masters Overland Stage was not a sound, firm investment for any bank. Jed did not let the objections come. He crossed to the window. 'Look out here and you won't refuse me.'

The bank manager rose from his chair and

joined Jed beside the window. 'See all those men, they're booking passages on my stage. I've promised to get them to Blackfoot Canyon as quickly as possible. I need another stagecoach and two men to drive for me and that needs cash.'

The bank manager paused for a moment and then, realizing that even if there was not a gold boom Jed would make money out of the immediate situation, he hurried to his desk.

'I'll arrange for an immediate loan right now.'

'Thanks,' smiled Jed, relief showing in his eyes. 'Let me sign the documents now then you can fix it up.'

The bank manager had already laid two papers on his desk. He signed them both then passed them to Jed for his signature.

'Sufficient to buy one stage and some on deposit for me to draw on as wages if necessary. I'll tell Jes Cutler he can draw the cash from you for the coach.'

'Leave it to me, Masters,' agreed the bank manager.

When Jed left the bank he recrossed the road to the agent's office. He saw at a glance that the agent had got everything well organized.

'Know where I can find two men to drive stage for me?' queried Jed.

The agent puzzled for a moment. 'Try the livery stable,' he suggested. 'Vance Wells and Mel Lockhart are often around there, they're interested in anything with a bit of life in it, especially if it is connected with horses.'

'Thanks,' replied Jed and hurried away along the sidewalk.

Two blocks further on he turned through the huge, wooden double-doors of Jes Cutler's wagon and coach building yard. The middle-aged, moustached man greeted Jed amicably and the transaction for the coach which Cutler had finished only a week ago was completed. Jed, satisfied with the way things were going, had one more call to make before he joined Dave in the *Gilded Cage*. He found Vance Wells and Mel Lockhart helping out at the livery stables.

They were younger than he had expected and judged them to be about the same age as his brother. They were both well-built, broad-shouldered and powerful for their age. They eyed Jed casually as he walked towards them.

'You fellers interested in driving stage for me?' he asked.

'Could be, depends on your proposition,' drawled the red-headed, sharp-featured Vance whose brown eyes took in Jed in one searching glance.

Jed explained his proposition quickly and precisely.

The blue eyes of the dark Mel met those of Vance and exchanged an agreement to take up Jed's proposition.

'When do you want us to start?' drawled Mel casually.

'Be at Jes Cutler's in half an hour, I've just bought a new stage and I'll be there with a team of horses.' The two men nodded. 'Just one thing,' added Jed, 'I hope you're going to stick with me and not take this as an easy ride to Blackfoot Canyon.' Instantly he regretted his words when he saw the reaction in Vance and Mel. He could see they were not just annoyed but they were hurt by his suggestion of mistrust.

'We aren't ones for breakin' our word,' snapped Vance. 'If you don't trust us then you'd better get someone else.'

'Sure,' added Mel. 'We don't see any fun in hackin' at a mountain hopin' it will spew gold at you, and we can always stay here if you...'

'I'm sorry, boys,' cut in Jed. 'I didn't mean anything. I've had so much on my mind lately, there was a possibility of having to give up the stage-line, but now this gold strike could save it I just don't want to see anything go wrong with my plans. I'm mighty glad to have you and I know you'll do all you can to make this a success.'

Vance smiled. 'See you in half an hour.'

Jed nodded, 'Thanks.'

As he turned to leave the livery stable the two men raised their hands in casual salute. Jed was in a happy frame of mind as he hurried to the *Gilded Cage* to find Dave Harman.

Bart Naylor was standing at one end of the long, highly polished mahogany counter in the *Gilded Cage* when Dave walked through the doorway.

Bart prided himself on his establishment saying that he could cater for all tastes. He was a tall, well-built man who held himself erect. His dark hair had a natural attractive wave which enhanced the clean-cut handsome features. He was an observant man whose dark eyes seemed to have a fascinating penetration. Elegantly dressed in a grey suit and an embroidered, fancy waistcoat he had a cravat neatly tied and pinned at his throat. He was a smooth operator who had come to Denver from Boston. He had seen possibilities in the town, opened the *Gilded Cage*, furnished it elegantly and attractively. At one end of the main room was a stage from which an entertainment twice a day amused the customers. The opposite end of this huge room was occupied by a small restaurant. The rest of the floor space was occupied by gambling tables which gave way to small tables for customers who just wanted to drink and watch the show.

The *Gilded Cage* had a good supply of customers throughout the day but at night it was always crowded. Bart Naylor made huge profits, was a generous boss and held a certain influence in the town, although some of the leading citizens suspected his motives and actions. A number of shady deals had been linked with Naylor's name but nothing could be proved and the talk passed off as rumours.

When Naylor saw Dave enter his establishment he immediately identified him as the lucky man. He pushed himself away from the counter and threaded his way between the tables towards the door.

'Guess you must be the man who's drained the *Gilded Cage* of most of its customers,' he said amicably with a friendly smile.

Dave grinned. 'Guess so.' He took Bart's extended hand and felt it gripped warmly in a friendly handshake.

'I'm mighty pleased to shake the hand of a man that's struck it rich,' flattered Bart. 'Maybe some of that yellow dust will rub off on to me. Well I think this calls for a celebration. Come on, the drinks are on me.'

He put his arm around Dave's shoulder and started to lead him to the bar.

'Hold on, Bart,' said Dave. 'I really want something to eat.'

'All the better,' replied Bart heartily. 'You'll have the best champagne dinner I can provide.' He piloted the bearded man towards the restaurant.

Dave was flattered by the fuss and revelled in the reception given to him by the owner of the *Gilded Cage*. Already he was enjoying the reflected power of his strike. Bart pulled out a chair for him and waved two of the waiters over. They responded instantly to his beckoning and Dave saw that he would get the best attention possible.

'See that Mr Harman gets everything he wants and charge it to the house. Make sure he gets my special champagne.'

The waiters nodded and hurried away to attend to everything.

31

'How do you know my name?' asked Dave.

Naylor smiled. 'There's not much goes on in Denver that I don't know about. I make it my business to find out and I was curious about the man who drew everyone out of the *Gilded Cage*.'

Dave grinned. 'Smart feller.'

'By the way,' went on Naylor smoothly, curious without pressing. 'Is your strike really as good as it sounds?'

'Look here,' replied Dave. 'You're being generous to me so I'll show you.' He pulled his leather bag from his pocket and Bart grinned to himself thinking how easy Dave was going to be. Dave tipped the contents on to the table. 'There you are!' he announced proudly.

Bart's eyes widened. He had not expected to see nuggets like this. It certainly looked as if the old man had hit a bonanza. Bart let out a long, low whistle. 'They sure are beauties,' he commented, as he picked up a nugget and examined it.

'Going to head for Blackfoot Canyon?' asked Dave.

Bart laughed. 'Me? Not likely. Strikes like that only come now and again. I could do an awful lot of digging and come out with nothing. My gold mine's right here.'

'Maybe you're right,' said Dave gathering up the nuggets. 'But there are a lot of folks out there who wouldn't agree with you. This rush is certainly goin' to save Masters Overland Stage if they play their cards right.'

'It should become a gold mine it itself,' quipped Naylor.

'Jed Masters will be joining me later if that's all right by you,' said Dave.

'Sure,' replied Bart and turned to the main body of the saloon. 'Enjoy yourself.' His quick brain was already turning over a number of ideas and by the time he reached the bar he had already formulated his first plan.

He called to the barman and when he arrived he told him to inform Luke Anson and Laura Peters that he wanted to see them in his room. The barman nodded and went in search of them whilst Bart hurried up the wide staircase and entered his own private room which opened off the balcony.

The room was large and elegantly furnished, reflecting the tastes of a man brought up in the 'smart set' in Boston. He lit a cigar and paced the room whilst he waited. A few minutes later the door opened and a small, dark, portly man came in. Bart had just offered him a drink when Laura Peters joined them. She was smartly clothed in a long tight dress which showed off her admirable figure. Her features were smooth and of a distinctive mould. Men would not describe her as pretty but as glamorous. Her great asset was her personality which seemed to strike to every corner of the *Gilded Cage* when she sang from the stage. Her red hair spoke of a quick temper which only Bart Naylor knew how to calm in an instant.

'What's the cosy chat for?' she asked as she crossed the room.

'We could hit the jackpot after our chat as you call it,' said Bart enthusiastically. 'I reckon you two can play it smooth enough to pull it off.' He told them about Dave Harman and how he had set him up for them. He went on to explain his idea and a few minutes later Luke Anson and Laura Peters left Bart's room convinced that before many minutes they would have pulled off a great scoop.

Five minutes later they entered the restaurant, paused for a moment, as if looking for a table, then, as Dave, attracted by the elegance of the lady, caught their glance they smiled and seeing his acknowledgement they strolled towards him. Sensing Dave's feeling of surprise and embarrassment at the fact that he did not match their elegance Luke whispered to Laura, 'Flatter him, he's an easy take.' Laura smiled and nodded almost imperceptibly.

'Wal, I guess we've found him, Laura,' said Luke enveloping Dave with a warm friendly smile. 'You must be Mister Harman.'

'Sure, sure,' stammered Dave, already under the spell of Laura's personality.

'I am delighted to meet you,' said Laura smoothly. 'I said to Luke I really must see the man who had discovered such a rich lode of gold.'

'Wal, I ...I ...' stuttered Dave, surprised that these people should take this personal interest in him. Most people just wanted to get out to the mountains and dig.

'Was it really as rich as they say?' asked Laura.

Dave swallowed as she leaned towards him. 'Why, sure it was,' he answered hoarsely. His mouth felt dry and he reached for his glass of champagne and drained it in one gulp.

Luke smiled. 'Would it be presumptuous to sit with you?' he requested.

'Sure, sure, sit down, glad to have you,' replied Dave.

Anson held a chair for Laura and when she had sat down he waved for a waiter.

'Another bottle of champagne,' he said and sat down on Dave's right.

Laura smiled across the table at Dave. 'I don't suppose you have just one little nugget I could see. I've never had the pleasure before.'

'I've got them all, right here,' answered Dave proudly, patting his pocket. He was feeling in his pocket when the waiter brought the champagne and started to uncork it.

'Just a moment, Mr Harman, you must have a drink with us first,' said Luke.

Dave smiled. 'That's right kind of you,' he said.

The waiter poured the drinks and as he moved away Luke raised his glass. 'To a prospector who struck it rich.'

Laura raised her glass and with a twinkle in her eye added, 'And a handsome one too.'

Embarrassed by the flattery Dave reached for his glass and drained it once again. A knowing glance passed between Luke and Laura. As Dave put down his glass Luke filled it up again.

'Now, Dave, are you going to let me have just one little peep?' asked Laura.

'Sure,' said Dave and pulled the leather pouch from his pocket. He tipped the contents on the table in front of Laura. She gasped as the nuggets rolled on the white cloth. Her eyes widened with surprise and Luke was equally amazed. She looked up at Dave.

'These are wonderful...' She seemed lost for words.

'Sure are,' said Dave proudly and drank some more champagne.

Throughout the next twenty minutes Luke kept Dave's glass filled up and made sure he had to do it often. He, with Laura's help, kept the conversation on the gold and prospecting and they gleaned that this was not some isolated find but possibly part of a huge vein running through the mountain.

'You know, Dave,' said Luke seriously, 'I work for an organization which is very interested in mining and in helping prospectors with their strikes.'

'That's interesting,' said Dave. His voice was becoming a little slurred and his mind was not acting as sharply as it should have done.

'Yes, we realise that in lots of cases it would be impossible for the prospector to carry on on his own,' pressed Luke seeing Dave was now at a state where he could be talked into almost anything. He did not want to act too rapidly, he wanted to appear to be selling a genuine deal, but he reckoned two more drinks and Dave would be ready.

'You might find it difficult,' put in Laura. 'Have you made any plans yet?'

'Not yet,' answered Dave. 'I've only just registered my claim.'

'Wal, I think I can help you,' said Luke smoothly. 'My firm will make you an offer for your mine, you have no worries, enough money to live on for the rest of your life and...'

'I don't think I want to sell,' slurred Dave.

Luke nodded to Laura who picked up the bottle of champagne and topped up Dave's glass. She moved round the table closer to Dave and pushed his glass to him. She picked up her own and smiled charmingly at Dave.

'Here's to a long friendship, Dave,' she said softly. 'If you take that offer you and I could see a lot of each other, you would be around all the time.'

'Sure you could,' pressed Luke. 'With the sort of money my firm will pay you you'll have nothing to do but enjoy yourself.'

'But what would I have to do?' asked Dave. The full meaning of Anson's offer had not penetrated to his befuddled mind.

'Nothing, nothing at all,' said Luke. 'Just

sign a form making the firm the legal holders of the claim.' He pulled a sheet of paper from the inside pocket of his coat. 'Look, here's one. All you have to do is to sign it at the bottom.'

Dave peered hard at the paper, narrowed his eyes, as if to see better, then murmured, 'I can't read all that.'

'There's no need, honey,' whispered Laura huskily. 'I'll read it for you.'

She picked up the paper and pretended to read it. 'This is in order, Dave, if you sign it you'll be a rich man. I'd sure like to string along with you with all that dough.' She placed the piece of paper in front of Dave and Luke placed a pencil beside it.

'Sign that and you'll never regret your action,' pressed Luke enthusiastically.

'I don't know,' slurred Dave. 'Seems a pity to sell a gold mine after looking for one all these years. Couldn't I keep just a tiny bit of it?'

Luke laughed. 'I guess it's only natural you should want to do that so I'll tell you what I'll do. You can keep a five per cent interest in it as well. My firm won't like it but I'll get round them.'

'I think that's mighty generous of you,' put in Laura. 'Don't you, Dave?'

He picked up the pencil and Laura and Luke watched, eagerly anticipating the big rake-off they would get from Bart Naylor when they presented him with a document stating that Dave Harman had handed over all the rights in his claim to the Western Mining Company.

Dave laid the pencil down. Luke's face clouded with a touch of anger in it.

'What's the matter?' he demanded.

'Just wanna drink,' stammered Dave and picked up his glass.

Luke waited impatiently. He had this all set up, nothing must stop it now. Dave put the glass down and picked up the pencil. Laura and Luke leaned forward to watch him.

'Right here,' said Luke pointing at the bottom of the paper.

Before Dave's pencil touched the paper a hand came over his shoulder and snatched the document away.

'Not there, not anywhere, Dave!' Jed Masters's voice rapped harshly.

Taken completely by surprise, Laura looked up, astonishment in her eyes; Luke straightened, surprise and anger on his face as he glared at Jed.

'See here, you can't...' began Luke.

'I can and have,' snapped Jed.

'Hello, Jed,' said Dave looking up with an innocent smile on his face. 'Meet my two friends.'

'Friends!' replied Jed contemptuously. 'They are no friends of yours.'

'But they were goin' to make me a rich man,' protested Dave.

'Rich!' snorted Jed. 'Your riches lie in those mountains not on a piece of paper.' He glanced at the sheet in his hand. 'I thought so. Dave, you're signing away your claim for nothing!'

The harshness of the words seemed to penetrate Dave's bemused brain. He jumped from his chair. 'What!' he gasped and turned on Anson. 'You low-down...' He left the sentence unfinished as he struck out at Luke but Jed grabbed him.

'Not that way, Dave. Come on, just let's get out of here,' he said. Jed faced Anson. His face was grim, his eyes narrowed. 'I don't know you,' he snapped, 'but let me catch you trying this again and I'll run you in. I'm surprised at Laura tossing in with the likes of you.' Jed did not wait for any answers. He grasped Dave by the arm and hurried him from the *Gilded Cage*.

There was fury in Anson's eyes as he

watched the two men move away from the table. His hand moved to the inside pocket of his coat but he was prevented from drawing the gun by the restraining hand of Laura.

'Not that, Luke. It won't do any good,' she whispered. 'It would ruin any more chances for Bart.'

'Guess you're right,' he muttered and poured himself some champagne which he drank in one gulp. 'Now I guess we'd better see Bart.'

'He isn't going to like it,' said Laura.

They made their way through the saloon, up the stairs to the balcony where their tap on Bart's door was answered with a shout of 'Come in.'

Naylor who was sitting behind a big desk smiled when he saw who entered the room. He rose from his chair and stepped round the desk to greet them.

'That would be simple enough for you,' he started but the words faded on his lips when he saw the serious expressions on the faces of Laura and Anson. 'Don't tell me you bungled it!' he gasped.

'Wal … we haven't got the paper signed,' muttered Anson, feeling ill at ease.

Bart's face darkened. 'Then you bungled it,' he said curtly.

'No, Bart,' put in Laura quickly, thinking an explanation by her might ease the blow. 'We didn't bungle it, we had him all set up, the pencil was in his hand, when that stage-line owner, Jed Masters, interfered and stopped Harman signing.'

'Masters!' Bart's voice was thoughtful trying to recall the man. 'I know him. Comes from Boulder. What had it to do with him?'

'Seems he is a friend of Harman,' replied Anson, pleased that Laura had turned Bart's anger.

'Then Masters will have to pay for what he's done.' The words hissed from Naylor's lips boding ill for Jed Masters.

'I'm sorry, boss,' put in Anson. 'But there was nothing we could do. He didn't know me so I reckoned it was best to keep quiet.'

'True,' replied Bart. 'It's just too bad Masters arrived when he did. Harman told me he was expecting him; I should have warned you, then you would have put the pressure on sooner.' Naylor was a fair man and he saw that to some extent he was to blame for the slip and that Laura and Anson had done their best. His face was thoughtful as he paced the floor. 'Pour yourself a drink, Laura. Luke, have a cigar.' He paused against his desk and picked up a box which he opened and handed to Anson. After he had selected a cigar for himself he lit it and restarted his pacing. 'Masters owns a stage-line exclusive rights between here, Boulder and Blackfoot Canyon. It was on its last legs but this gold boom will sure put it in the money. I reckon we can get our own back on Masters.' He had been voicing his thoughts rather than talking to anyone, but suddenly he stopped and turned sharply to face Luke. 'The agency for the stage-line is across the street, mosey over there and see if you can learn anything about Masters' plans, and be as quick as possible. Laura, get Carl Frome for me.'

As Laura and Luke closed the door behind them, Bart Naylor sat down in an easy chair.

'Clever Mr Masters will have to be taught that it doesn't pay to interfere with Bart Naylor,' he muttered to himself.

3

Five minutes later there was a knock on the door of Bart Naylor's room and a burly man in a faded brown shirt tucked into the top of blue jeans walked in. His Colt was slung low and thonged round his thigh. His dark hair was untidy and he carried a battered, black sombrero.

'You wanted to see me, boss?' he drawled, pausing just inside the door.

'Yes, come right in, Carl. I have a job for you and the boys. They haven't gone gold hunting I hope.'

'Nope,' answered Carl as he moved forward, his appearance in marked contrast to that of Naylor.

Bart detested untidiness, but in Carl he had recognized a man not afraid to use the strong-arm, a man used to using a gun and a man afraid of no one. Whilst he had not the subtleties of Naylor's thinking, Bart knew him to be a man of integrity, a man who would not reveal who his boss was, not even to his own riders.

'Good,' replied Bart. 'I hope the gold fever won't get hold of them.'

'It won't,' grinned Carl. 'They reckon there'll be easier pickings comin' along with this boom.'

'How right they are,' mused Naylor half to himself. 'Pour yourself a drink, Carl,' he added, indicating the decanter on the table.

Carl muttered his thanks and it was whilst he was filling his glass that Anson returned.

'Got the set-up?' asked Bart.

'Sure have. It appears this here Masters is going to cash in on this boom. He's bought himself another stagecoach, hired a couple of drivers and is going to run a shuttle service between here and Blackfoot Canyon by way of Boulder. There's a great queue booking passages now.'

Bart nodded, his fingertips pressed lightly together in front of his lips. The thoughtful look on his face indicated a mind toying with a plan. Both men watched him without speaking.

Suddenly he looked up. 'Thanks Luke.' The two words acted as a dismissal as well as an appreciation. Luke left the room without a word and Bart waited for the door to close before he spoke. He always deemed it a wise precaution that the fewer people who knew his plans the better.

'Carl, I want one of those coaches, preferably the new one, wrecked,' instructed Naylor. 'That will put Masters in a spot; no doubt he's borrowed the money to buy it and he'll be hoping to make it pay by transporting men to Blackfoot Canyon.'

Carl grinned. This was the sort of job he liked. 'We'll fix it, boss.'

'I want it doing so it appears to be an accident. Make out you're excited men on your way to find a fortune,' said Bart.

Carl nodded. 'Leave it to us. The accident will probably take place over Sioux Pass.'

When Carl left the *Gilded Cage* he paused to watch Vance Wells driving the new stagecoach up to the agency. He stopped amidst loud cheering from the would-be prospectors, and the agent stepped forward to usher the correct bookings on to the stage. The older coach was already full and Mel Lockhart was awaiting Jed's order to move out. Jed gave some instructions to Vance and told him that he would be able to catch them up. 'We'll let you take the lead; it will give Clance a surprise to see a new coach rolling into Boulder.'

The coach had filled quickly and Jed waved it away. With a flick of the reins and an easing of the brake, Vance set the stage in motion. He swung out past Mel who yelled at his team of six and followed Vance. A loud cheer went up from the crowd as the first two stage-loads of men, hoping to find their fortunes in the new diggings around Blackfoot Canyon, got under way.

Jed watched with a certain pride and, as the two coaches neared the end of the street, he turned to his agent.

'Keep up the good work at this end,' he said. 'I'm going to take my horse and ride with the coaches.'

Jed hurried to the stable at the back of the agency where he always kept a horse in case either he or Clance should need one when they were in Denver. He saddled the animal quickly and was soon riding after the stage-coaches.

When Jed moved out on the trail from Denver he was amazed at the number of people on the road. The magical attraction of the word gold seemed to be drawing all men to that great backcloth of the Rocky Mountains purpled by the distance, rising tier upon tier reaching seemingly to the very heavens. This was a sight which never failed to thrill Jed whenever he made the trip back to Boulder from Denver. There was a challenge in the great barrier and now it threw out another invitation – gold. Men were on foot, their few belongings strapped to their backs; mules and horses offered an easier means of transport to others, whilst wagons were filled to overflowing. Any means at all was used in the urge to get to Blackfoot Canyon.

But Jed's mind was not on the gold but on these men, he saw them as the saviours of the stage-line. Whatever freight had needed to be hauled before, he had managed with the coach and the occasional hiring of a wagon. Now, he and Clance were going to have to think big about the freight-hauling side of the business. Men meant materials and food and that meant he would need wagons. He should have thought of this whilst he was in Denver but he had been preoccupied with the new stage and Dave Harman. Maybe he should turn back and see Jes Cutler about some wagons, but he wanted to ride into Boulder with the stages, the first trip in the new life of the Masters Overland Stage.

Jed pushed his horse into a faster pace and before long the coaches, billowing dust behind them, came into sight. Vance Wells had drawn about a quarter of a mile ahead of Mel Lockhart but now the stages were matched in a pace which covered the ground quickly. Jed frowned; were these two twenty-one-year-olds going too fast? At this pace things would easily get out of hand unless they were used to handling teams of six horses. The natural exuberance of the passengers must have over-ridden the caution of the drivers. Jed tapped his horse into a gallop, bent on cutting down the speed of the coaches. The trail began to rise gently and the dust was left behind as the wheels gripped at the harder surface. Jed was not far behind the coach driven by Mel Lockhart and was about to urge his horse faster in order to come alongside when he held back. The trail had narrowed and at the pace the coach was going it required skilful handling on the part of the driver. This, Mel Lockhart was doing with the utmost ease and Jed recognized in him someone used to handling horses in spite of his young years. Jed felt easier in his mind and spurred the horse faster to pass the coach in order to check on Vance Wells.

He waved to Mel as he passed and soon found that his new coach was being handled equally skillfully by Vance. Jed now matched his pace to that of the coach and rode about a hundred yards to the rear, convenient to the two coaches should he be required for any purpose.

The road climbed and twisted; mountains closed in upon it, seeming to dwarf the coaches as they headed for Sioux Pass to surmount the first barrier in their path. For the last mile of the climb the road hung precariously on the great mass of rock with a huge drop on one side. The horses toiled hard pulling the laden coaches, but even they sensed the ease they would feel once the top was reached. The descent was not quite as steep, but there were more bends, needing skilful handling of the teams by the drivers, but, by now, Jed had no fear that Vance and Mel could cope with the situation. Jed relaxed in the saddle his mind dwelling on the future.

Vance's coach was almost at the top of the pass when Jed was suddenly shaken out of his dreaming by the thrum of hooves behind him. Some folks were sure anxious to start their search for gold sending their horses up this incline at this pace. He turned in his saddle to see six men bunched together as if in a race. They were yelling at the top of their voices filled, supposedly, with excitement in the rush. Jed grinned to himself, marvelling at the effects a gold-find could have on men. One of the riders pulled a gun

51

from his holster and fired into the air. The sound reverberated from the wall of rock and was thrown across the narrow valley. This brought a yell of satisfaction from the man and he continued to fire into the air. Other riders followed suit, creating a great frightening noise across the pass. They were close to Jed and he felt his horse twitch uneasily at the noise. He called to it soothingly and held it firmly in check, nevertheless the animal was clearly uneasy.

The riders thundered past and Jed cursed them for their unconcerned stupidity. Suddenly, alarm seized him. His coach was at the top of the pass swinging over the crest ready for the downward trail. If those fools scared those horses the first trip could end in disaster; an uncontrolled run from the top of Sioux Pass could result in nothing else.

Jed kicked his horse into a gallop and raced after the men, not knowing what he could do to stop them but instinctively having to do something.

Vance Wells adjusted himself on the seat of the coach and controlled the six horses firmly, preparing them for the down-hill run. He loved the feel of the reins in his hands, delighted in working with animals, loving every minute of the ride. The crash of gunfire behind him caused him to stiffen and, as it was repeated and drew nearer, some measure of concern seized him. He glanced round anxiously, to see six riders, firing their guns in the air, coming up fast.

'Fools!' muttered Vance, as he felt his horses react nervously.

Suddenly, it seemed the riders were alongside yelling excitedly and still firing into the air. Vance's horses were scared and broke into a faster run. His yells at the riders went unheard or unheeded and he turned his concentration to controlling the horses which were tugging at the reins in their effort to get away from the frightening sounds around them. Vance fought them in an effort to keep some control to prevent the dead run of an uncontrollable team. The ground spun beneath the flashing hooves as the horses strained every muscle against the reins and harness. Black manes streamed in the wind as the coach achieved a frightening speed. Alarm seized the occupants, yells came from inside, whilst those on top clung grimly to the iron luggage rack to prevent the sudden ejection into space, by the sway of the coach, becoming a reality.

The coach was swaying precariously as the first corner seemed to fly at them. Vance tried to check the onrush, but his attempts had little effect on the horses. Then they were into the corner, the horses were round and the coach skidded towards the edge of the trail. Wheels screeched on the hard ground; the coach swayed towards the drop then it was round and racing down the incline towards the next bend.

To Jed, racing behind the coach, it looked as if it was bent on certain destruction. The riders who had caused the trouble had passed the coach and were galloping ahead but two seemed to slacken pace, whooping and yelling, and as the coach caught them up they continued to fire their guns. Jed, anxious to catch the coach, was watching Vance, hoping he would still be able to keep the horses under some sort of control. Suddenly, anxiety gripped Jed when he saw Vance fall sideways. Jed yelled at his horse and kicked it harder. The animal answered his call and stretched its run. Jed saw Vance struggle back to the sitting position and fight the pull of his team. The riders had gradually out-run the coach but Jed had no eyes for them. It seemed to him that he would never gain on the swaying, bumping stage.

Then they were into the next corner. It seemed to the passengers that they were certain to plunge to their doom but somehow the coach stayed upright and they were round the corner with a thunder of hooves and a scream of iron.

Jed put his horse at the corner close to the rock face and turned it sharply, cutting it as much as he dare to gain a few precious yards on the coach. Then he was alongside, moving faster, overhauling the horses inch by inch. As he drew alongside the front of the coach Jed glanced up anxiously at Vance and he saw pain as well as anxiety, courage and determination in the young man's eyes. Jed was level with the second horse as they were flung into the left-hand turn of the next bend. Destruction threatened to come from the wall of rock on the right as the coach swayed and skidded towards a vicious contact. There was little between the wheels and rock as the coach came out of the corner.

The incline steepened towards the next bend, and Jed knew the coach must be slowed before it reached the corner, nothing could save his new vehicle if it went into the bend at an increased speed. Desperate measures were needed. As he drew alongside the lead horses he edged his own horse nearer. Flaying, death-dealing hooves flashed beneath him. Jed eased his feet from the stirrups, judged the distance, as he pulled his horse close to the team, and flung himself out of the saddle. His arms reached for the harness, his hands grasped for support. Jed's body crashed against the animal, his fingers gripped the leather and as he fell across the horse's back he straddled it. The body was heaving beneath him, plunging on towards destruction. Jed gripped with his legs, and hauled hard on the harness. The horse fought against the pull trying to keep pace with the horse alongside.

Vance supported Jed all he could, by fighting the team with the reins. The muscles in Jed's arms and shoulders stood out against the weight of the rushing animals. They screamed out for release from the torture but Jed kept hauling hard on the harness. The bend seemed to be rushing at them with no decrease in speed. Jed tugged harder and began to feel some response to his efforts in spite of the resistance of the horse. Gradually he felt the speed slacken and with its coming Vance experienced more control through the reins, but still the ground flashed beneath the pounding hooves. Then they were upon the corner. The coach swayed and was flung out-wards away from the turn in a screeching skid. For an awful moment Jed thought they had not managed to slacken the speed enough. The wheels ground along the edge, and with the tug of the six horses the coach was suddenly whisked away from destruction.

Jed experienced a sense of relief but he knew the fight was not over yet. With a long straight stretch of trail before them he and Vance had time to gain complete mastery of the team. Gradually they brought the stage to a halt. Steam rose off the panting horses. When he was sure they were quiet Jed relaxed his aching muscles and found relief when he swung to the ground. The passengers had poured from the coach as soon as it halted and were in the process of helping Vance down from the top of the stage. Jed hurried to the group and it was then that he saw the blood on the fleshy part of the arm just below the shoulder.

'You all right?' asked Jed anxiously as he reached him.

Vance nodded. 'Sure,' he said. 'It's just a scratch, fortunately.'

'Those damn fools,' said Jed viciously. 'They should have had more sense.'

'They sure made a good effort to get us over the edge,' remarked Vance.

Jed shot him a hard glance. 'You think it

was deliberate?'

'Don't you?' countered Vance.

'Didn't give it a thought,' replied Jed. 'Put it down to high spirits due to gold.'

Vance looked thoughtful. 'You could be right but I…' He stopped in the middle of his sentence as if doubting that what he was about to say was true.

'Go on,' prompted Jed.

'I could be wrong,' said Vance.

'Never mind, say what you were thinking,' urged Jed, his curiosity aroused by the implication lying behind Vance's unspoken thoughts.

'Wal, I didn't get much of a chance to have a look at them, I was taken up tryin' to control the team, but I thought I recognised some of Carl Frome's side-kicks, an' I don't think they'll be interested in gold, at least gettin' it the legal way.'

'But why should they want to wreck the coach?' said Jed.

'I don't know,' replied Vance, 'I thought you might be able to answer that one.'

Jed shook his head thoughtfully. He knew of Carl Frome by reputation but he could think of no reason why he should be behind an attempt to wreck the stage, if indeed that was what it was.

As if suddenly remembering the needs of his passengers he turned and called out, 'All aboard, we'll roll again now.' He glanced at Vance. 'I'll tie my horse to the back and ride up top with you.' Jed hurried to his horse which had followed the stage, and after securing it, he climbed up beside Vance and took the reins.

'You know,' he remarked, 'I can't think why anyone should want to wreck the stage. I think you must be wrong.' Nevertheless Jed could not dismiss the idea sown by Vance, and it was a serious, thoughtful Jed who drove the stage the rest of the way to Boulder.

The pending excitement drove these thoughts from Jed's mind, when the small town, with its magnificent background of the majestic mountains, came in sight. Clance was going to get a surprise when two stages rolled into Boulder.

There were few people about when they reached the main street and Jed guessed that the men had already forsaken the town for the lure of gold. The pound of the hooves brought Clance Masters hurrying from the stage office. His blue eyes widened with surprise when he saw two coaches approaching. Who was running another stage into Boulder? His mind had automatically put up a protestation against someone else moving in on their rights. Then he saw his brother.

Jed was grinning at the bewildered look on Clance's face as he pulled to a halt in front of the office.

'Hi there, little brother, how do you like our new buy?' he shouted as he jumped down from the driving seat.

'Ours?' gasped Clance. 'But ... what...'

'Tell you all about it in a minute,' called Jed over his shoulder as he helped Vance down to the sidewalk.

'What's been happening?' asked Clance, his curiosity sharpened by the sight of Vance's wound.

'Nearly lost this coach,' said Jed. He turned to the occupants of both coaches who were clustered on the sidewalk. 'This stage will leave for Blackfoot Canyon in twenty minutes. We'll take you in one load if you don't mind the crush and some more of you will ride on top.' The would-be gold diggers shouted their approval and dispersed to pass away twenty minutes in the saloon. 'Hi, Mel, come over here,' called Jed. When Mel joined them Jed introduced him and Vance to his brother. 'Employed them to drive our coaches,' explained Jed. 'Mel, this may not be much of a town but we do boast a doctor. You'll find him further along the street. Take Vance and have that wound looked at.' When the two young men walked away Clance turned to his brother.

'Now, what's all this about?'

'It's going to be boom time for us,' explained Jed. 'You saw those folks on those stages, well there are a lot more making bookings in Denver. I realised if we were to cope with the demand we needed another coach. I borrowed the money from the bank and closed the deal. I figure we can run a shuttle service between Denver and Black-foot Canyon with Boulder as the turning point.'

Clance was warming to Jed's enthusiasm. 'You think this is the real thing then?' queried Clance.

'Well even if it isn't there are still going to be a lot of folks to transport out here and back; that should pay for the coach. If it is a boom we'd better think big and get in with the freighting as well.'

Clance grinned. 'You've sure got it all worked out, and to think only this morning I was trying to talk you into selling the business.'

'This is just what pa dreamed about,' said Jed. 'Come on, Clance, we'll change the team on the new coach, it's had a rough run.'

'What happened?' asked Clance.

Jed told him the story as they changed the horses.

'They sure could have cost us a lot of money,' commented Clance at the end of the tale.

'It would have finished us,' said Jed. 'We would never have paid off the debt on the new coach with only one operating and we certainly wouldn't have been able to borrow any for freighting wagons.' He paused, then added thoughtfully. 'I wonder if there was anything in Vance's idea that it was deliberate?'

'Deliberate?' Clance was surprised.

'Yes,' replied Jed and when they entered the office he went on to relate what Vance had said.

'But who and why?' queried Clance.

'I don't know,' answered Jed.

Their conversation was interrupted by a knock on the door and the appearance of Dave Harman.

'Hi, boys,' he called as he shut the door. 'I just want to thank you Jed for what you did today.'

'Think nothing of it, Dave. Just be careful in future. Remember, we are here if you want any help,' said Jed. 'Are you feeling all right now?'

'Sure,' grinned Dave sheepishly. 'That ride back cured me, but I'm mighty glad I took the old coach from what I hear. Whose takin' us on to Blackfoot Canyon?'

'I reckon Clance will,' said Jed.

'See you on the stage,' said Dave as he left the office.

'What's he on about?' questioned Clance, his curiosity raised by the conversation.

Jed told him the story quickly. Clance was thoughtful when Jed finished.

'Could there be a connection between this and the attempt on the stage?' he queried.

'Why should there be?' replied Jed, surprised by Clance's implication.

'Wal, you'd just spoilt the deal.'

'But those riders went right on past me, didn't even try to get at me,' answered Jed.

'Killin' you wasn't on their books but gettin' at you through destroying the stage-coach was.'

'That could tie in with Vance's idea,' said Jed thoughtfully. 'That would mean the hombre called Anson hired Carl Frome's side-kicks, but Anson was a stranger to me.'

'There are a lot of people in Denver we don't know,' pointed out Clance. 'You told

63

me he had Laura Peters with him. Now Laura is Bart Naylor's girl so what was she doing with Anson? Could Naylor be behind this?'

Jed gave a low whistle. 'Steady on Clance, you're digging deep. I reckon Naylor has been behind some shady deals but nothing has ever been proved and you'd have a hard time pinning this on him. Best forget it.' He pushed himself to his feet. 'Come on, let's get the stage rolling.'

They reached the door just as Vance and Mel arrived. Vance was disappointed that he was not going to drive the coach but Jed insisted that he should rest his arm for a couple of days.

'Clance will take the coach to the canyon and Mel, you hit back for Denver, change teams there and bring out another load of prospectors. One more thing,' he added, 'both of you watch out for any more trouble. I don't think we'll have any, but its best to be on your guard.'

The two men nodded, checked their coaches and, in five minutes, were pulling out of Boulder in opposite directions.

4

In the busy weeks which followed all thoughts of a possible enemy were driven far from Jed's thoughts. Everything went smoothly. With untiring effort three runs a day were fitted in and on every trip the stage was packed. Mel and Vance fitted in perfectly with Jed and his brother and they became intensely interested in the welfare of the stage-line.

Boulder had mushroomed in that week. Hundreds flocked into the town; a tent city grew up on the south side, and buildings were hastily erected extending the main street and developing new ones. Boulder just could not cope with the invasion and at times chaos reigned. Blackfoot Canyon was littered with tents marking a small area where a man hoped to find his fortune and leave for ever the rough life he was experiencing.

For a whole week the only man to take gold out of the mountain was Dave Harman and he was cautious about it. He knew how easily the lust for gold could warp men's minds until they could see nothing else and would go to any lengths, even murder, to satisfy their greed. But Dave took precautions. Only Jed knew of the exact location of his find and when Dave returned to the mountain he skilfully laid false trails in case anyone should be shadowing him. When he came out of Box Canyon he did so with the utmost caution and was even more cautious when he returned.

Then two men struck gold far up Blackfoot Canyon and a new gold rush was on, strengthened by the finds of another four men in the same canyon the following day.

The hundreds turned into thousands and Boulder's tent city grew to huge proportions, bringing with it all the hangers-on of the roughness of a mining town. Everyone seemed to be out to make an easy dollar.

With the coming of the new rush Jed and Clance realised they would have to expand the freighting side of the business quickly. They had been reluctant to do so until a big boom was certain. Their freighting methods were already taxed to breaking point with the first influx of people but now, with the new strikes, the position was impossible unless they bought new wagons.

The decision taken, Jed accompanied Mel on the stage for Denver. Jed enjoyed the journey, revelling in the opportunity to relax for a while after the hectic time of the past week. After arriving in Denver, Jed checked that all was well with his agent and then visited Jes Cutler from whom he bought two wagons. There was no difficulty in borrowing the money from the bank, and it was a satisfied Jed Masters who sought out Mel Lockhart when the deal was completed.

'I've just bought two wagons, Mel,' Jed informed his stagecoach driver, 'now I want four men to handle them and the freight. Think you can find any?'

'I reckon so,' replied Mel.

'Good,' said Jed. 'One of them must be able to take the responsibility of buying the necessary goods if the occasion arises. Normally Clance or I will handle it but there might be times when we can't. I'll be in the *Gilded Cage,* bring them there.'

Mel nodded and hurried away and Jed crossed the road to the saloon. Whilst he was having a drink at the bar Bart Naylor sauntered up to him.

'Good day, Masters,' he said amiably as he leaned on the long counter.

Jed nodded. Whilst he really had nothing

personal against Naylor there was something about the man that he did not like.

'Reckon these gold strikes have saved the Masters Overland Stage; I believe you hadn't a great deal of trade before,' said Bart.

'I guess we were lucky,' replied Jed curtly.

'Things will be booming in Boulder now,' said Bart. 'The number of people who have passed through here makes me think that Boulder's the place to make money. If the boom continues Boulder will become an important town.'

'Reckon so,' agreed Jed.

'Then book me a place on the stage today,' said Bart.

'You'll have to do it through my agent,' replied Jed.

'I'm doing it through you,' insisted Bart.

'It may be fully booked,' answered Jed sharply offended by Naylor's air of superior authority.

'Then unbook a place for me,' rapped Bart between tight lips.

'Sorry,' said Jed, 'I can't do that. If it is booked when I get to the office then you will have to wait your turn.'

'Look here, Masters, don't cross me; I'm a man of some influence in this town and if I move into Boulder I could make things unpleasant for you.'

'You threatening me?' questioned Jed, annoyed that someone was trying to dictate to him.

'Just see that I have a seat on that stage,' hissed Bart and walked away.

Jed watched him, wondering just how far the man's influence went and what form it took. Jed found his thoughts turning to the near loss of his new stagecoach. He wondered if there could be anything in the theories of his brother and the suspicions of Vance Wells. Today was the first time he had had any wrong words with Bart Naylor. Maybe Naylor had been irritated by the loss of a gold mine, if indeed he was behind Anson's attempt to get the mine off Dave Harman.

Jed's thoughts were interrupted twenty minutes later when Mel Lockhart arrived with four men about his own age. As he was introduced to them Jed mused on the fact that he was building up a young team and wondered if they would be able to cope with trouble if it came. He dismissed the thought immediately, remembering Vance's handling of that first stage ride, and also because he respected Mel's judgement. Mel gave their names as Sam, Tay, Buck and Red, naming the latter as the man he reckoned would fill Jed's requirements of wagon foreman.

Jed liked the look of them. Sam, Tay and Buck were big framed, muscular, young men with open friendly faces, but Red was the man who stood out amongst them, not that he was bigger, in fact if anything he was thinner and not so broad shouldered. He was a tall angular man, his jaw jutted prominently from a brown weather-beaten face, but it was his flowing red hair which caught Jed's eye immediately he took off his grey sombrero.

'We're mighty glad to be with you, Mr Masters,' said Red. 'The boys here nominated me foreman so to speak if that's agreeable with you.' There was a keen, friendly, sincere look in his brown eyes.

Before Jed could speak Mel put in, 'Red's father owns a freighting business back in St Louis.'

'Then what are you doing here?' queried Jed with surprise.

'There's nothing wrong, Mr Masters,' Red was hasty to explain. 'I wanted to come west, father said it would be a good thing for me and the freighting business is waiting for me if I want to go back to it. Guess this job will give me some experience, although naturally I've had some with my father.'

'Then you fit my job admirably,' said Jed thanking his luck. 'And no more of the Mister, I'm Jed to you all.' He called for drinks and explained his ideas to them.

After they had finished their beer they left the *Gilded Cage*. Mel went to the agent's office to check the return trip to Boulder whilst Jed took his four new employees to Jes Cutler's. Jes had the wagons and horses ready for them and whilst Sam, Tay and Buck checked everything over, Red accompanied Jed on a buying expedition. Food, ammunition, implements for mining, timber, nails and everything required for the building trade were ordered. Jed instructed his foreman about rates of payment and the arrangements with the bank.

'We'll sell this load in Boulder. A second store has already sprung up there and there'll be others to follow. Future loads will consist of specific orders from the people in Boulder and we'll just make freighting charges,' explained Jed, 'but it's no good wasting a trip to Boulder.'

He left Red to see to the shipment and made his way to the agent's office. As he approached the office, outside of which the coach was drawn up, Jed could see there was some trouble. Pushing his way through the small crowd which had gathered, Jed saw Mel arguing with Bart Naylor and he knew immediately what the trouble was about. Behind Naylor, Jed saw Carl Frome and wondered if he was there to back Naylor up.

'Something wrong, Mel?' asked Jed casually.

'Mr Naylor insists that he booked a seat through you but the agent knows nothin' about it an' the stage is full for this run,' explained Mel.

Jed looked hard at Naylor. 'I told you I couldn't accept the booking, you had to do it through my agent. I'm sorry Mr Naylor, you'll have to book for a later stage.'

'Couldn't or wouldn't?' snapped Bart, annoyed that Jed had not knuckled down to his authority. 'What have you got against me?'

'Nothing,' answered Jed testily. 'I run a stage-line and no matter who wants to use it they must book in the proper manner or there would be chaos. You're a businessman Naylor, you should know that.'

'I've got to get to Boulder,' said Bart irritably. He knew Jed was right but he would not admit it. 'It's vitally important.'

'Any one of these passengers could say the same thing,' answered Jed.

'I warned you, Masters.' There was an undertone of threat in Bart's voice.

'You'll take Mr Naylor!' Carl Frome took up Bart Naylor's attitude towards Jed, but there was more menace in his voice.

'Neither you nor anyone else will tell me what to do,' hissed Jed his eyes narrowing with anger.

Carl's hand had moved almost imperceptibly towards his gun. Suddenly it moved swiftly over those last few inches and closed round the butt of the Colt, but before the weapon cleared its leather Carl found himself staring into the cold muzzle of Jed's Colt.

'Don't try that,' warned Jed. The icy implication in his voice left no doubt in Frome's mind as to the outcome if he tried to draw his gun. 'Ease your hand off that butt,' ordered Jed. Carl, his face dark with annoyance, did as he was told. 'Now, Naylor, take your pet monkey and git back to your saloon. If you still want to go to Boulder check with my agent after the stage has left.'

Naylor hesitated for a moment but under the threat of Jed's gun reluctantly turned and, followed by Frome, pushed his way through the crowd.

The silence which had come upon the crowd was now broken and everyone started to talk at once.

Jed turned to Mel. 'C'm on let's get the stage rolling.' He pushed his Colt back into its holster and mounted the stage. Mel clambered up beside him, picked up the reins and with a flick and a shout set the horses in motion. As they moved away Jed glanced back at the two men on the sidewalk outside the *Gilded Cage*. 'Know of any previous association between Naylor and Frome?' he asked Mel.

'No,' came the answer.

'Vance thought they were Frome's sidekicks that nearly caused the stage to be wrecked and now Frome backs up Naylor. Could there be a connection?' mused Jed.

It was just the sort of theorising which was causing Naylor some concern at that very moment.

'It would have been better if you hadn't interfered, Carl.' There was irritation in Naylor's voice. 'It is possible that we'll be linked now.'

'I'm sorry, boss,' said Carl, 'but I thought...'

'Oh, it doesn't matter, I suppose,' cut in Naylor. 'None of your past activities can be traced back to me and we'll keep it that way in future, it's just that Masters might put two and two together and get nosey.'

'Then Masters will have to be dealt with,' said Carl, the tone of his voice leaving no mistake as to his intentions.

'Come on Carl,' said Naylor, 'we don't need that stage to get us to Boulder. When Bart Naylor gets organised in that town the Masters Overland Stage and its owners can count its days.'

The two men crossed the street to the *Gilded Cage*.

'Get our horses ready, Carl, Jed Masters won't keep us out of Boulder today.'

Carl nodded and left Bart Naylor for the stables. Bart hurried to his room in the *Gilded Cage* and changed quickly into his riding outfit. A blue shirt topped a pair of black trousers tucked neatly into the top of shining, black riding boots. Bart tied a brown neckerchief round his throat, and donned a matching vest. He buckled a gun belt around his waist and holstered his pearl-handled Colt.

When he returned to the main street Carl Frome was waiting with two horses. As he stepped down from the sidewalk to take the reins, he glanced along the street and saw two wagons rumbling out of Jes Cutler's yard.

Naylor swung into the saddle but held his

horse in check whilst he watched the wagons moving slowly along the dusty street.

'Someone looks as though they are setting up in business,' commented Naylor. 'Any idea who?'

'No,' replied Carl.

Naylor pushed his horse forward at a walking pace when he saw the wagons draw up outside one of the town's stores.

'Launching out into the trading world?' queried Bart as he stopped beside the first wagon.

Red glanced round and was surprised to see the speaker was Naylor. 'No, not me,' he replied. 'We are working for Jed Masters.'

'I see,' smiled Naylor. 'I thought it might be you and was just going to wish you luck.'

'Thanks,' replied Red. He watched the two men, as they rode slowly away, puzzled that Bart Naylor should take an interest in him. The second wagon stopped and Sam and Tay joined him, interrupting his thoughts.

When Bart Naylor and Carl Frome reached the end of the main street they put their horses into a quicker pace.

'Jed Masters is moving fast,' commented Naylor. 'A new stage and now two new wagons for freighting, he's making the most of this boom. I was just going to look Boulder over but, if the prospects are good, I'll have to move today otherwise Jed Masters can become too much an influence there.'

'Any time you want that coyote dealin' with just say the word,' was Carl's laconic comment.

5

When Mel Lockhart started to bring the coach to a halt in front of the stage-line's office in Boulder, Jed Masters, seated on top of the coach, was surprised to see Bart Naylor amongst the crowd awaiting the arrival of the stage.

As soon as the coach stopped Jed swung to the ground to be greeted by his brother.

'Good trip?' queried Clance.

'Sure,' answered Jed. 'Has everything been all right here?' he added, suspicious of Naylor's presence.

'Yes,' replied Clance and busied himself with the transference of the passengers to the stagecoach which was ready for the journey to Blackfoot Canyon.

Jed helped Mel to change the team ready

for the trip back to Denver. Bart Naylor leaned against the wall of the office and watched the activity with amused interest.

When everything was ready Jed called to Clance. 'I want to see you before you go.' His brother waved his acknowledgement and Jed turned to the office. As he reached the door Bart Naylor stepped forward.

'Hi, Masters. I didn't need your stage to get me to Boulder after all,' said Naylor with a grin.

'So I see,' replied Jed testily.

'You seem to have a pretty thriving business now,' commented Naylor casually. 'Add the expansion of your freighting unit to it and you have plenty to keep you out of mischief.'

'I hope you have plenty to do as well,' snapped Jed. 'You've evidently been nosing around before you left Denver.'

Naylor grinned. 'And I've been having a look round here,' he said. 'Matter of fact I've just bought the *Golden Nugget* and the property alongside it.'

Jed's eyes widened with surprise at this announcement. 'You sure don't waste any time.'

'I don't,' agreed Bart. 'Now what about the Masters Overland Stage – care to sell that?'

'I would not,' replied Jed coldly.

'I'm serious about this, Masters,' said Bart firmly. 'Let's go inside and discuss it; I'll make you a very good offer.'

'Nothing doing,' answered Jed. 'The business is not for sale.'

'I think there is someone else who should have a say in the matter,' said Bart when he saw Clance approaching. 'I believe your brother has a share in the business.' Jed did not answer and, as Clance joined them, Bart greeted him warmly. 'I've just been making your brother an offer for your stage and freighting business.'

'I don't think we're really interested,' said Clance, reading a refusal in Jed's eyes, 'but as a matter of interest what was your offer?'

'I hadn't made it yet,' replied Naylor, somewhat taken aback by Clance's casual attitude. 'I suggest we go inside and discuss it.'

'I don't think we need bother, Naylor,' drawled Clance. 'Your offer couldn't come up to our demand – there's a great potential here and, by rights assigned to my father, no one can operate alongside us, so you see we hold a very valuable business.' He pushed past the two men and entered the office.

Jed smiled. 'There's your answer, Naylor.' He followed his brother, leaving an ill-tempered Naylor glaring at the door as it shut.

'Thanks,' said Jed. 'You said just the right thing out there.'

'I guess Bart's goin' to feel a bit sore,' grinned Clance.

'I reckon we're going to have to keep our eye on that hombre,' said Jed. 'He's just bought the *Golden Nugget.*'

'What!' gasped Clance. 'It looks as if he wants to get firmly established in Boulder same as he did in Denver.'

'Yes,' agreed Jed, 'and you know the rumours that flew around there regarding some of his deals.'

'But nothin' could be proved,' pointed out Clance, 'and he's respected by a lot of the leading citizens.'

'Sure,' said Jed. 'I reckon he'll try to do the same here. I ran foul of him in Denver today; thought he could grab a seat on the stage.' Jed went on to tell Clance what had happened.

'Well, I reckon we'd better brief Mel and Vance to be on the look-out in case there's trouble brewin',' said Clance at the conclusion of Jed's story.

'Do that,' said Jed. 'I've put us deep in debt by purchasing two wagons. We can't afford for anything to go wrong.'

Throughout the next week things went smoothly. The regular trips between Denver and the mines were all full and the brothers were delighted at Red's handling of the freight side of the business. That first consignment was sold before it was off the wagon and from that moment on the wagons were kept on the move hauling supplies into Boulder. Even Bart Naylor gave the Masters Overland Stage the job of bringing in timber and everything else necessary for the enlarging of the *Golden Nugget*.

Bart did not have any personal contact with the Masters brothers, but he was extremely busy consolidating his position in Boulder. He went ahead immediately with his plans for the *Golden Nugget* whilst keeping it open. He bought up other property and it was rumoured that, whilst the main store was still operated by Zeke Chambers, it really belonged to Bart Naylor. The man from Denver was seen with all the leading citizens of Boulder who had started to take an interest in the town. With the arrival of the boom Boulder was growing fast; it was obviously going to be a place of the future and as such had to be organised and run properly.

The tent city and the influx of so many

people led to problems, not the least of which was law and order and it was this situation which led to a meeting of the leading citizens being held in the *Golden Nugget* with the object of electing a sheriff.

On the morning of the meeting Jed was working in his office when the door opened to admit two men, both of whom were in their late fifties. Bud Peters and Frank Carr had both come to Boulder about the same time as Jed's father. Bud owned a great deal of the land in and around Boulder and it was obvious that he was going to make a lot of money out of land deals. Frank had a ranch a few miles east of Boulder and if the town grew there was going to be plenty of call for more cattle. He also owned the town's only hotel and immediately a boom was certain he had put forward plans for expansion and another building was being converted for more hotel space.

They greeted Jed warmly and he indicated chairs for them.

'I'm sure glad to see the stage-line thriving,' said Bud. 'Your father would have been thrilled.'

'He sure would,' agreed Frank. 'He always had faith in this place.'

'This boom was just what was wanted for

Boulder,' said Jed, offering the two men cheroots.

When he had lit his cheroot Frank looked seriously at Jed. 'Of course it's throwing a lot more responsibility on to the people who have been here a long time. We've got our mayor and sort of council to run things, not that there has been much to see to, but now it's a different matter, we'll cope all right, but what is important is to see that a strong lawman is elected tonight.'

'Quite so,' put in Bud. 'With the great influx of people it is necessary, an' with the rowdyism an' such like coming in with the tent city, an' believe me some of the goings on over there want stamping out, we must have a good sheriff.'

Jed was rather amused at the way these two were talking without coming to the point. Although they had been contemporaries of his father he was not particularly friendly with them and he knew there was something behind this visit.

'Gentlemen, I am just as aware as you are of the necessity for a good sheriff. Law and order established with a firm hand right at the start can keep this town free from trouble which follows a mushroom growth on riches.' Jed paused. 'Now, gentlemen, I am very busy at this time so please come to the point.'

Peters and Carr exchanged glances. They had hoped to pass this off as a social call but the younger man had caught them out.

'Wal,' spluttered Peters, 'the point is, will you be at the meeting tonight?'

'Yes,' replied Jed.

'The real point is, we wondered if you had anyone in mind for the job,' said Carr.

'I have,' answered Jed, 'but I don't think I am prepared to discuss it.'

'Come now, Jed, we aren't exactly strangers. If some of us get together over this I think it will save a lot of time and we can be sure of getting the right man in,' said Carr.

'That depends who you have in mind,' replied Jed warily.

'We're prepared to discuss it if you are,' said Carr.

Jed hesitated a moment. He felt he would like to keep his own counsel but at the same time, he could not help feeling that there was something more to this visit; besides it would be advantageous to know how these men were thinking. All sorts of schemes could be afoot especially when so much money would be circulating in Boulder.

Jed nodded. 'All right, who have you got in mind?'

'Wal, we figure Mike Kilner to be the best man,' replied Frank. 'He's a good man with a gun, he's been in Boulder quite a while and he's handled a sheriff's job in Missouri.'

Jed's face did not betray his real feelings at this choice but he did not temper his words. 'What you say is true,' he said, 'but we don't know why he left that post in Missouri.'

'Came into some money so there was no reason to carry on,' pointed out Peters, 'but I'm sure he'll take this on, he has the interests of Boulder at heart.'

'Maybe,' said Jed quietly. 'There was a robbery in Missouri about that time – not far from the place in which Kilner was sheriff.'

'You don't believe he had anything to do with the robbery,' Frank Carr was surprised at Jed's insinuation.

'He came here with plenty of money, he's never worked since...' Jed paused, shrugged his shoulders, then went on. 'I've nothing to go on really, but my real objection is that I believe he is a man who can be easily led, whereas we must have a man with a firm hand. In a town the way this will grow, all sorts of bribes could be slipped to the sheriff. Our man must be a man of the utmost integrity, otherwise chaos can reign.'

'I'm sure Mike Kilner will fit these specifications,' said Peters firmly.

'So do I,' affirmed Carr.

'Well, I'd be happier with Walt Cooper,' said Jed.

'What!' both men gasped together. 'Walt backed down from a gun-fight over in...' went on Bud quickly. 'We couldn't have that happen here. If a sheriff backed down the bad element would run riot. Since comin' here he's done nothing but help out at the livery stable.'

'That's nothing against him,' pointed out Jed. 'He's as straight as anyone can be. There'll be no messing with Walt Cooper, if he had a sheriff's badge on everyone would be treated alike.'

'But what would happen if he had to face a gunman?' said Bud derisively.

'He'd shoot it out and in all probability beat the gunman to the draw, Cooper's fast, very fast. Gentlemen I'm going to tell you something now which only I, in Boulder, know. Walter asked me to keep his secret but I think in the interest of Boulder and in his own interest I should tell you, because I'm certain he's the man who should be sheriff. The man from whom Walt backed down was his own brother. Walt knew he was the better shot, knew he would kill his own brother and couldn't do it. He ruined his own prospects and he lost the girl he loved. His brother was killed a month later but he had killed another four people in the meantime. Walt blamed himself for their deaths and the whole thing preyed on his mind. That's why he keeps so much out of the way. All he needs is a job like this to win back his self-respect.'

Both men were surprised by this story. 'All this may be true,' said Peters, 'but it seems to me you're acting on sympathy for Walt Cooper.'

Carr nodded his agreement. 'And that's a point, Jed, we can't afford to let sympathy creep in. The position of sheriff, especially at this time, can't be used to experiment with a man's life. We've got to be certain of our man. We can't be certain of Cooper but we can of Kilner.'

'I'm not acting on sympathy,' said Jed. 'I am sure Cooper's the man we want.'

Carr's lips tightened. 'I'm sorry you can't see it our way, Jed.'

'You'll be running against the general feeling if you nominate Cooper,' added Bud Peters.

'Then you know how people are going to

vote,' said Jed curtly.

'No, no.' Peters was just a little too hasty with his denial for Jed's liking. 'We've talked to several people, it's just a feeling we have.'

Before Jed could reply Frank Carr pushed himself to his feet. 'Come on, Bud, we'd better be going or we'll be late for our appointment.' He glanced at Jed. 'Think things over before the meeting, son. It's better we all back the same man.'

Jed did not reply but merely nodded to the two men and watched them leave the office. He must have sat nearly five minutes, pondering over the interview, before he moved. He had no reason to believe that Peters and Carr were genuine in their approval of Kilner for sheriff but something rankled at the back of his mind. Suddenly he jumped up and hurried from the office. Maybe he'd better do a bit of canvassing on Walt Cooper's account even though Walt did not know what was in Jed's mind.

At seven-thirty that evening Jed and Clance entered the *Golden Nugget*. They had half an hour to spend before the meeting so they positioned themselves at the bar so that they could see the whole room. A few minutes later Bart Naylor sauntered over and greeted them amicably but with no real warmth.

'Glad to see you,' he said. 'All set to elect a good sheriff?'

Jed nodded. 'The best.' But he did not reveal who he had in mind. He wondered if Naylor already knew that.

'How do you like what I'm doing to this place?' asked Naylor, not wanting to appear too keen to pursue the question of the new sheriff.

'Fine,' said Jed.

'Looks as if you are going to model it on the *Gilded Cage* in Denver,' observed Clance.

'That's right,' said Bart. 'That paid dividends and I reckon this will.'

'There's no doubt about it, it will,' agreed Jed. 'So why try to buy us out, you've enough to keep you occupied here?'

Bart smiled. 'Business. You've got to be enterprising today.' He glanced across the saloon and before either of the brothers could make a remark he added, 'Excuse me, gentlemen. There's someone I must see.'

Jed and Clance watched him as he moved away. 'Greed more like it,' muttered Clance. 'He wants to rule the town. He'll have to be watched, Jed.'

'He sure will,' agreed Jed. 'I guess he's already using his influence to good effect,' he added when he observed Naylor greet Bud

Peters and Frank Carr and escort the two men to the rooms at the back of the saloon. 'Clance, I had a feeling there was more to the visit made by Peters and Carr this morning. It's my guess that it's really Naylor who wants Mike Kilner as sheriff, a man like Kilner who can be easily led would soon be under Naylor's influence. No doubt he's made promises to Peters and Carr for their support.'

'Sounds feasible to me,' said Clance.

'I'd sure like to know what's going on in that back room now,' said Jed. He straightened suddenly. 'I'm going to see if I can find out. Wait here for Walt Cooper.'

Before Clance could say anything Jed hurried away. He went through to the back of the saloon and found himself in a dimly lit corridor from which four doors led to rooms on the right. Jed moved quietly along the corridor, paused against the first door, but hearing nothing he moved on to the second. No sound came from that room, but when he reached the third door he recognised Carr's voice.

'I tell you he's been around pluggin' the case for Cooper. He's well liked around Boulder and I reckon we're not goin' to have an easy time gettin' Kilner into the job.'

'Kilner's got to be sheriff!' Jed stiffened as he recognised Bart Naylor's voice. His suppositions had been right. 'You two put me on to Kilner, and if he's elected to the post we're made. I'll have him eating out of my hand. He'll shut his eyes to many things, the town will be ours and with it a fortune.'

Jed could feel the intense excitement in Naylor's voice. Naylor was prepared to do anything to fulfil his ambitions. The rumours about his activities in Denver must be true but there was no proof, just as there would be none here in Boulder. Jed's immediate impulse was to throw open the door and face the three men but he realised that would be useless. They would laugh at his accusations and deny them because he had no witnesses. But now Jed was armed with knowledge of the association.

'But what about Masters?' There was concern in Peters's tone.

'He could be a nuisance,' agreed Naylor, 'but there are ways and means of dealing with the likes of him, but first of all we must get Kilner elected.'

Jed figured he had heard enough. He turned and walked quietly away and re-entered the saloon, taking care to make his entry inconspicuous. As he crossed the saloon he saw that Walt Cooper was with Clance. After he had exchanged greetings Jed, keeping his voice to undertones, related what he had overheard.

'What are we goin' to do?' asked Clance.

'There's nothing we can do at the moment; the important thing is to get Walt elected sheriff. Clance, circulate and push his case as much as you can before the meeting.'

As Clance moved away, Walt looked hard at Jed. 'I came here determined to tell you not to put my name on the nomination, but after what you've told us I'm with you all the way.'

'Thanks,' smiled Jed. 'I thought you would be.' He slapped the tall, broad-set Cooper on the shoulder. 'Just hang on here until the meeting.' Jed crossed the room to a group of men sitting round a table and, when he walked into Bart Naylor's room at the back of the saloon a short while later, he felt a little happier but not altogether confident. He realised there would be a lot of talking to do.

After the nominations had been made and Walt Cooper and Mike Kilner had assured the meeting they were willing to accept the position of sheriff if elected they left the room and returned to the bar. Both men leaned on the long mahogany counter and called for a beer. Throughout the next hour neither spoke to each other, both, dwelling on the situation, were lost in their own thoughts. Occasionally the sound of raised voices came from the back room; it was obvious to the two men that their nominations were the subject of heated discussion and argument.

Both men were getting uneasy when the door opened and a small portly man who held the office of mayor led the meeting into the saloon. Walt Cooper and Mike Kilner straightened from the counter and turned to face the group.

'Walt Cooper,' the little man stepped forward, 'I have to inform you that you have been elected Sheriff of Boulder.'

Walt could hardly believe his ears. Congratulations were showered upon him. He glanced beyond the mayor to Jed, who nodded his congratulations with a faint smile, but Walt could tell from the serious expression on his face that it had been tough going to get him elected.

'All the best.' Walt was aware that Mike Kilner had taken his hand in a friendly grip.

'Thanks,' said Walt.

The mayor pinned the badge of office to Cooper's brown shirt and handed him a bunch of keys. 'Those are the keys to the old office and jail. This could be a tough job with Boulder growing as it is, hope you can manage it, Walt.'

'I'll do my best,' drawled Walt, somewhat embarrassed by the trust which had been placed in him.

Bart Naylor appeared from the back of the saloon and called out. 'I figure we should drink the new sheriff into office – it's on the house.'

A great cheer went up and people swarmed round the bar. Twenty minutes later Walt Cooper, accompanied by Jed and Clance, left the *Golden Nugget*. The night was dark but a glow from the numerous kerosene lamps of the tent city filled the sky and a few lights shone from houses further along Main Street. The three men walked slowly along the sidewalk.

'It was touch and go wasn't it?' said Walt.

Jed did not speak so Clance explained. 'It sure was. First of all Jed challenged Naylor's right to be there. That more or less split the meeting in two but finally there was something of a compromise; Naylor could stay but not note. A good job he couldn't otherwise we would have had a stalemate; you got in by only one vote, Walt.'

Cooper let out a low whistle. 'Things could

be rough if I don't get a good backing.'

'They could,' agreed Jed, 'but I don't think that a vote for Kilner necessarily meant support for Naylor, but he's a smooth talker and blinds some of them with what he can do for Boulder. Maybe he can, but it will mean he runs the town, and some of them can't see that. Walt, that old sheriff's office hasn't been used for years; you can put a desk in ours until you get it cleaned up.'

'Thanks,' said Walt gratefully, 'but I won't do that. I'd rather move in there right away, it will help to strengthen the symbol of my authority. In fact I'd like to have a look at it now.'

'I understand,' smiled Jed. 'Clance, can you get a lamp from the office?'

'Sure,' replied his brother.

'I'm mighty grateful for what you've done,' said Walt appreciatively. 'I'd lost faith in myself, now I feel that some of it has been restored. I only hope I can do a good job.'

'You will,' affirmed Jed.

Clance returned with the lamp. 'We'll go along with you,' he said. 'You should have a welcoming committee at your office.'

The three men crossed the dusty roadway and mounted the opposite sidewalk. Their footsteps echoed as they hurried to the long-deserted office which stood about fifty yards from the end of the street. Walt fumbled with the keys whilst Jed searched for a match to light the lamp held by Clance.

Suddenly the night was split by the crash of a gun. Woodwork splintered where the bullet tore into the doorpost, narrowly missing Walt and Clance. Instinctively the three men dived on to the sidewalk, their hands reaching for their Colts. There was a noise across the street and footsteps beat a tattoo on the wood as someone ran along the sidewalk. Jed raised his Colt and fired. There was no one to be seen. Whoever the would-be assassin was was keeping to the shadows and the darkness of the night did not help matters. It was more in hope than judgement that Jed fired again, but still the footsteps sent their mocking echo across the street. Walt fired and this time there was a pause in the steps before they continued at the same pace as before.

Clance leapt to his feet. 'I'm goin' after him.'

'Hold it!' yelled Jed scrambling up. 'You won't do any good. Listen, whoever it is has left the sidewalk.' A faint plod came to the three men. 'He's gone up some alley. He could be anywhere by the time you got over there.'

Clance shrugged his shoulders. 'Guess you're right.'

'Wal, seems as though I don't meet with someone's approval,' drawled Walt.

'And it shows what lengths they are prepared to go to,' pointed out Jed. 'You'll have to watch your step, Walt.'

6

Mel Lockhart eased himself on the seat of the stagecoach. He held the six horses to a steady pace, conserving their energy for the rougher going three miles ahead on his way to Boulder from Blackfoot Canyon. This was one of his easiest journeys for all he was carrying were four miners returning to Boulder, disillusioned in their search for riches.

Mel reflected on the big changes which were developing in Boulder and how the Masters brothers had expanded from a one-stage outfit with little call for it into a thriving stage and freight line with immense potentialities. His thoughts turned to the new sheriff who, after only two weeks in office, was making a name for himself. He had cleaned up some of the seamier sides of the tent city and stood no nonsense from the itinerant miners. He was even stricter with the hangers-on, the leeches of a gold boom, and endeavoured to protect the miners from the greedy grasps of such people. Never once had he used his guns, though no doubt he would do so if forced. He had used his fists and on one occasion had walked right up to a belligerent gun-waving miner and disarmed him. He was earning a great respect in the town.

Mel was jerked suddenly out of reverie when a man staggered from behind some rocks into the path of the coach. Mel hauled hard on the reins, his right foot clamping hard on the brake handle. The wheels screeched tortuously as they slid on the hard surface. The coach swayed and skidded. The horses fought the sudden resistance but Mel's strong wrists held them in check. The horses seemed to be on top of the man before he was aware of him. He staggered sideways and Mel was never sure whether the lead horse brushed him or not, but he saw the man fall clear of the flaying hoofs. The coach came to a halt a few yards beyond the prone figure. Mel leapt down from his seat and raced back, shouting to his passengers to come and help.

As he dropped to his knees beside the man Mel was surprised to see the bullet-furrow high on his temple and blood soaking his shirt from an ugly wound in his side. The four miners from the coach joined Mel.

'Give me a hand to get him in the coach,' said Mel urgently. 'He needs a doctor quickly.'

As they started to lift the man his eyes flickered open. 'Wait, wait,' he said weakly. 'I'm done for but I must tell you...' His voice faded, then he seemed to gather strength from somewhere as Mel cradled his head more comfortably. 'They got us both,' he went on, his words coming slowly and spasmodically and then sometimes in a rush. 'The other's, over there.' Mel nodded to one of his passengers who hurried over to the rocks beside the trail. 'We were bringing our gold back, they got the lot.'

'Who were they?' asked Mel.

'Dunno. Four of them, masked. Forced us off the trail, we made a run for it. Killed Charlie; reckon they left me for dead.'

'Can you tell us anything about them?' pressed Mel.

'They were... Were...' The words seemed to choke in the man's throat. He made one last effort and fell back in Mel's arms.

The passenger returned a few moments later to report that the other body lay about thirty yards from the trail amongst a group of rocks.

It was a grim-faced Mel Lockhart who pulled the stage to a halt in Boulder. He was glad to see Walt Cooper standing with Jed Masters outside the stage office.

'Two miners have been robbed and killed ways back,' he said as he faced Jed and Walt.

Their smiled greeting vanished and they exchanged astonished glances.

'I've got them in the coach,' added Mel.

The sheriff issued orders for the removal of the bodies then turned to Jed. 'Can we go inside? I want to know all the details from Mel.'

'Sure,' answered Jed.

When Mel had finished his story Walt looked hard at Jed. 'I wondered when this sort of thing would start. I didn't like the miners bringing in their gold themselves.' He looked thoughtful for a moment. 'Jed, have you ever been asked to carry gold on the stage?'

'No,' replied Jed. 'You know what these miners are, hate anyone to handle their gold until its safely deposited, even then some of them are suspicious of the bank.'

'Wal, if robberies are goin' to become frequent – and, havin' got away with one, these men won't stop – we're goin' to have to do something about it,' said the sheriff, 'and I propose we do it right away before there's any more killin'. These miners will have to ship the gold on the stage or we can't be responsible for protecting them.'

'It means I'm going to have to provide shot-guns,' said Jed.

'Any objection?' asked Walt.

'No,' replied Jed. 'I only hope you can persuade the miners it's the thing to do.'

'I'm goin' out to Blackfoot Canyon right away,' said Walt. 'Will you ride along?'

'Sure,' said Jed. 'We'll discuss the set-up as we go, then we'll have something to put before them.'

Ten minutes later the two men left Boulder at a quick trot and headed for Blackfoot Canyon.

A short distance from the end of the canyon a gathering of tents and shacks had sprung up which formed a base for the hundreds of diggings spread throughout the canyon and along the mountain sides. There were about fifty men at this base when Walt and Jed rode in and the sheriff soon had the word spread around that he wanted a meeting of everyone for four o'clock in the afternoon and that he would like as many of the men from the diggings as possible to attend the meeting.

There was a bigger gathering than he had expected when Walt stepped on to the top of a big boulder. When Walt informed the miners of the robbery and killing a wave of consternation ran through the gathering. As the murmuring subsided Walt continued.

'In order to prevent any more killings of this nature I propose that you ship your gold into Boulder through the Masters Overland Stage. I have Jed Masters here with me now, his service is efficient and he has agreed to co-operate in this matter.'

'The stage can be held up; if we carry our own money we can and will fight to keep it,' yelled one man.

Jed jumped up beside Walt. 'I will provide a man to ride shot-gun on the stage. Apart from him there will be the driver and the passengers – all added protection for your gold. My men will be briefed to do anything to prevent your gold being taken. I will set up a place here to which you can bring your gold, it will be well guarded and we will not ship gold on every stage. By this means the robbers will never know which stage is carrying gold. Occasionally I will provide extra men to ride along, in this way the hold-up men will never know what opposition they will meet – it will act as a deterrent to them.'

'We urge you to think seriously about this. If you want this scheme to operate we'll do it, but it needs your backing or it is no good organizing it,' Walt shouted. He hesitated a few moments when murmurings broke out as the miners began discussing the project amongst themselves. 'Right, can we take a vote on it?' he shouted. 'All those in favour of supporting such a scheme.'

There was such a display of hands that there was no need to ask for dissenters. The crowd began to break up and when Jed jumped down from the boulder he found himself confronted by the warm smile on the friendly, bearded face of Dave Harman.

'Hi, Dave, it's good to see you,' grinned Jed, slapping the older man on the shoulder. 'How are things with you?'

'Fine, son, fine. I'm mighty glad to see you,' said Dave, giving Jed a friendly blow on the chest. 'Guess you're doin' all right.'

'Sure. I've expanded, so I am not showing much profit yet, but it will come. How about you, still digging it out?'

'Yep. I've got it all stacked away up in the mountains. One day I'm pullin' out an' never comin' back; that day I'll need your stage.'

'It will be yours,' grinned Jed and bade farewell to the old man.

In two days Jed was all ready to start receiving gold and shipping it out to Boulder. He based Clance and a guard in a shack in Blackfoot Canyon and he hired two men to work turns riding shot-gun.

For a week all went well. Two shipments of gold were made without mishap. Even though they had voted in favour of the scheme the miners were still somewhat reluctant to part with their gold, especially those who had not come in from their diggings to the meeting. However with the successful conclusion of the two journeys gold began to flow in.

The third shipment proved to be a big one and although Jed would have liked to have been along, a big freight shipment from Denver took him back to Boulder before the shipment day. He decided therefore to leave things as normal so that no more attention was drawn to this shipment than either of the other two.

Mel felt a little nervous as the stage pulled out of Blackfoot Canyon but, with a shot-gun and four passengers all armed and briefed, he soon lost the tension once they were under way. He kept the horses to a quick pace and his eyes alert for any danger which might be ahead. All went well for four miles but, as they approached a point where the trail narrowed through boulder-strewn hillsides, Mel warned his shot-gun to be extra alert.

'This is a likely place if anything is to happen,' he called.

The shot-gun nodded and eased the rifle in his hands.

In spite of their vigilance they were caught completely unawares when four horsemen suddenly appeared alongside the coach, two coming on each side. Automatically Mel yelled to his team and flicked the reins to send the animals into a gallop. But almost at once he had to haul hard on the reins as two large boulders came crashing down the hillside on to the trail a short distance ahead. The man beside him had instinctively brought his rifle to his shoulder at the appearance of the masked riders but before he could fire a bullet crashed into his chest, sending him crashing from the coach. Two of the horsemen had fired rapidly into the coach, rendering any return fire ineffectual.

The stage came to a stop. Mel glanced

round desperately and, seeing the situation was hopeless, raised his hands slowly.

'Git down,' ordered one of the riders harshly.

Mel clambered out of his seat and, when he reached the ground, he saw two men, holding wounded arms, stumble out of the stage.

'The other two are dead,' muttered one of them.

Mel was horrified. Three men killed, two wounded and their resistance had been so ineffectual that not one of the robbers had been harmed. One of them swung down from his horse and roughly disarmed Mel and the two passengers, whilst another climbed on to the coach and passed down the three boxes containing the gold. The locks were shot off and in a short time the gold was transferred to the saddle-bags. Whilst all this was going on Mel studied the men intently, but there was nothing by which he felt certain he could identify them. Horses and clothes could be changed and their features were well covered up. Mel was in despair, he had fallen down on his first big shipment. He tried in vain to see some loophole in the robbers' vigilance. He was almost driven to try something desperate but his common sense prevailed. He would be gunned down without mercy and he figured he was better alive than dead. It was with a heavy heart that he watched the masked men ride away.

As the dust swirled behind the riders, Mel examined the two wounded men. They had not been badly hit and said they would be able to help Mel push the boulders off the trail. Once these had been cleared they collected the shot-gun's body and placed it in the coach with the others. The three men climbed on to the coach and Mel sent the horses forward.

When Jed Masters saw the stagecoach hit the main street of Boulder at a fast run he knew something was wrong and when he saw the three men on the top instead of the usual two his fears were confirmed.

Mel pulled the coach to a dust stirring halt. 'They got us,' he yelled.

Red, Sam, Tay and Buck left the wagons which they were unloading and ran to join Jed. The unusual approach of the stage and Mel's shout had attracted other people and soon there was a crowd gathering round the coach.

'What happened?' called Jed almost before the stage had stopped.

'Hold-up,' answered Mel as he jumped down. 'Hadn't a chance, they got the lot. Three of us killed and two wounded.'

Jed gasped. This was a severe blow to the stage-line. He frowned. 'Tell me about it inside.' Eager hands were helping the wounded men from the coach. 'Tay, get the two men to the doc. Sam, Buck, see to the bodies. Red, get the sheriff.' Jed's instructions were sharp and concise and the men set about their tasks immediately. He led Mel into the office and the stage driver started to apologise.

'Forget it,' interrupted Jed. 'I know it was not your fault before you even tell me your story.'

'But I should have been able to do more,' said Mel.

'I know you would do exactly what the circumstances would permit. Now, forget about blaming yourself, otherwise it will affect your future driving.'

The door opened and Red walked in with the sheriff, who looked troubled by what little he had learned from Red. Mel told his story quickly, leaving no detail untold and the three men listened intently without interruption.

'Someone is keepin' tag on the shipments

from Blackfoot Canyon,' said Walt Cooper when Mel had finished his story. 'The first two were allowed to go through to lull you into a false sense of security. They knew when the big one was comin'.'

'We keep the day of the shipment a secret but once we start loading it would be obvious that a consignment was going out,' said Jed.

'Then someone is keeping an eye on things at Blackfoot Canyon,' mused the sheriff. 'Once he sees the shipment being made he tips off the gang. That means the gang must be hangin' out somewhere near the trail so that they can be in position quickly.'

Jed looked thoughtful. 'I guess you must be right,' he said. 'It's the only way it could be worked. In that case I can't see any connection with Bart Naylor, he's been in town all day; I've seen him around.'

'That doesn't mean he can't be connected,' pointed out Walt. 'He could be the brains behind this affair. You know, Jed, he's been quiet since I became sheriff, in fact he's co-operated in many ways – playing the model citizen – that could be a cover. You refused to sell the stage-line, which, with its exclusive rights, could really give power to an unscrupulous man, therefore attacks on the stage could have a double effect of grabbin' gold and forcin' you out of business.'

Jed nodded thoughtfully. 'Then he'll have a fight on his hands,' he muttered with determination. 'Now, I've got to ride out to Blackfoot Canyon and tell the miners.'

'I'll come with you,' said the sheriff.

'Mel, you take it easy for the rest of the day. Red will you take over here? As soon as the wagons are unloaded you can send them back to Denver, put Tay in charge. Warn Vance when he comes in about what has happened.'

When he was satisfied that everything had been dealt with, Jed and Walt left the office and were soon heading for Blackfoot Canyon.

The sight of Jed Masters riding into the camp with the sheriff did not arouse any un-due comment, for both men were often seen around, but when they walked into Clance's make-shift office he knew only trouble would bring Jed to Blackfoot Canyon at this time.

'Need we tell the miners yet?' he asked his brother.

'It's got to be faced, so better now than later,' replied Jed. 'There's no need to call a meeting once word gets around the miners will come clamouring.' He turned to

Clance's assistant. 'Start spreading the news.'

Jed's words proved true and before long a large crowd of miners had gathered, shouting for news, demanding explanations, calling abuse and enlarging on the natural rumours of inefficiency on the part of the stage-line. When the two brothers and the sheriff stepped out of the hut there was a great roar which took some minutes to subside after Jed had held up his hands for silence.

He gave the facts to the gathering quickly and concisely and concluded by saying, 'We hope you will continue to have faith in the stage-line and still use it to ship your gold.'

His words were lost in a roar of disapproval and it took some time to get the crowd quiet again, during which time several alternative suggestions had been voiced.

When the noise abated Walt Cooper stepped forward. 'This is the first time the stage has been robbed, you must give it another chance, it is still the safest way of getting your gold through. In future I will ride with the stage myself and I'm going to organize some armed riders to accompany it whenever it is carrying gold.'

The crowd was a little calmer now as they began to see sense in the sheriff's words. Sensing the beginning of a change in mood,

Walt pressed his case and in ten minutes the miners were persuaded not to forsake the stage-line. As the crowd dispersed Jed expressed his thanks to Walt.

'It's the least I could do after you got me this post,' said Walt. 'Can we arrange for your wagon team to act as riders whenever there's a shipment of gold?'

'It can be organised,' said Jed.

'It would be best if we keep this sort of thing amongst your men; we know them and can trust them,' explained Walt.

'There's no reason why I can't ride with the stage as well,' said Clance. 'Once it's safely through I can return here.'

'Good,' commented Walt. 'If they try another hold-up they're sure in for a rough time.'

7

It was a week after the hold-up when Bart Naylor sent for Carl Frome.

'I reckon we can work another raid on the stage,' said Bart. 'Three more stages carrying gold have come into Boulder and Walt

Cooper is still riding shot-gun. This gives us the opportunity we want.'

'It won't be as easy this time,' said Carl. 'Masters makes no disguise of the fact that a coach is carrying gold, he has patrols riding with it.'

'Don't let that worry you,' smiled Naylor. 'I've got it all worked out. You'll need more men, divided into two groups, one to create a diversion, the other to carry out the actual raid.' He went on to explain the idea in more detail.

Frome grinned. 'I'll fix it.'

'Good. There's only one instruction from me. You must ride with the hold-up party, and make sure the sheriff is killed.' Naylor grinned. 'Death in the course of duty. Make it look like that; we daren't risk it looking deliberate after that first attempt failed.'

Carl nodded. 'Leave it to me. We'll need a new sheriff in Boulder before long.'

Two days later news was brought by one of his men that a stage carrying gold but no passengers had left Blackfoot Canyon with a patrol of five men. Carl had already briefed his men as to their various jobs and they immediately made preparations to leave the hollow in which they were camped a short distance from the trail.

113

Unaware that they were under close scrutiny, Jed Masters, driving the stage, and Walt Cooper, riding shot-gun, approached a point a mile from the position of the last hold-up. Suddenly a volley of rifle shots from the hillside on their left cut through the noise of the moving coach.

Jed immediately put the horses into a faster pace and the five men who were riding patrol came together along the side of the coach nearest to the attack. Two horsemen appeared on the trail a short distance ahead, but, immediately they saw the number of men protecting the stage they pulled their horses round sharply and put them up the hillside in the direction of their companions who were still firing.

Clance sighted the two horsemen and with an excited yell of 'Come on, let's get them,' he turned his horse in pursuit. The other four riders followed, and immediately the rifle fire broke off. Three men broke from cover, scrambled on to their horses and set off up the rocky hillside.

'Sure looks as if our numbers frightened them,' said Jed. 'Your idea of patrols is working.'

'Don't be too sure,' commented Walt. 'They gave up a little too easily for my liking.'

Jed frowned; it was an angle he had not considered, but a mile further on, he realised how true Walt's suppositions were when four masked horsemen appeared on the trail beside them. The coach was already going fast but Jed urged the horses to more speed. Walt's rifle was up in a flash and his bullet hit one rider in the shoulder but, before he could fire again, a bullet took him between the eyes and he fell back across Jed's feet. A quick glance was all that was necessary to tell Jed that Walt was dead, but shock was lessened by his concentration and determination to out-run the riders. Already he had drawn ahead of them and he hunched himself down as much as he could as bullets whined past him.

The team was straining every muscle and were at full stretch when Jed saw two boulders rolling down the hillside towards the trail. Alarm seized him, the robbers were using the same technique as their last raid. Jed eyed the distance quickly but carefully. If he could out-run those boulders before they crashed in his path he might get away. There was a chance. Jed yelled at the horses, urging sweating bodies to greater effort. Their manes streamed behind them, their hooves flashed over the ground. The coach bounced and swayed behind them, every joint screaming with agony at the torturous speed. A doubt seized Jed; if he didn't get past, the horses would hurl straight into the boulders; there would be no stopping them in time. Jed estimated the distance. He thought he could do it and he kept the animals at full speed.

Then suddenly he was there; the boulders seemed to be hanging over him; the horses were past; he was past; then the world seemed to turn upside down and hit him. There was a sickening crash behind him as one of the boulders hit the back wheel. The coach slewed across the trail heeling over precariously. It hit the hillside and was bounced back. Jed felt himself leave the coach and the next thing was oblivion.

'Jed, Jed, can you hear me?' The anxious voice seemed far away. Jed's fogged brain could not grasp the situation. He was sure his eyes were open, there was a brightness but he could not make out the speaker. The voice continued urgently, pleading for recognition. A blur began to form before Jed's eyes, he made out the form of a man. His brain pounded, the words became louder; he recognised the voice.

'Clance.' The word came more as a croak but it was a joy to the man who was on his knees cradling his brother's head in his arm. 'Jed!' Suddenly Clance's face sprang into focus and Jed mustered a smile. A canteen of water was poured between his lips and he enjoyed the feel of the wetness. He saw feet around him and glanced up to see Red, Tay, Buck and Sam, concern on their faces, standing round him.

He struggled to sit up and managed it with Clance's assistance. His head swam and his body ached. He felt as if he had been kicked from head to foot. He sat still for a moment until his head cleared again, then he checked himself over and was thankful that he appeared to have nothing worse than a bad shaking and bruising.

'I just didn't make it,' he muttered.

'When we saw the coach and the boulders we guessed what had happened,' said Clance.

'The coach!' There was alarm in Jed's voice. 'Is it…?' He started to struggle to his feet and powerful hands helped him.

'It's over there, not too badly smashed, it is repairable. The horses are all right, but Walt is dead and the gold has gone,' said Clance.

'Walt was killed before we crashed and they would have an easy time getting the gold,' said Jed dejectedly. 'They tricked you into following and that left the coach almost undefended.'

'We realised that when we came back to join you,' muttered Clance angrily, annoyed that he had fallen so easily into the trap. 'And we didn't even get one for identification; they gave us the slip.'

'We'd better get back to Boulder,' said Jed. 'Unhitch the team, we'll take the horses with us.' Whilst Tay and Sam unfastened the horses the other three men examined the coach.

'I reckon if three of us came out with one of the wagons tomorrow we can repair it and tow it back into Boulder,' said Red.

'Good,' replied Jed, handing over the responsibility of the job to Red. 'Clance, you'd better ride back to Blackfoot Canyon, try to appease the miners, tell them I'll be out tomorrow and no doubt I'll have another sheriff with me; if I'm not mistaken Bud Peters and Frank Carr will press for a quick election of a sheriff and no doubt they will be pushed into this by Bart Naylor.'

Jed's words proved to be true for no sooner had the word of the new hold-up and the death of Walt Cooper gone around when Peters and Carr were urging a quick election of a new sheriff.

'We can't delay; a sheriff is essential in a growing town. Someone must get on the track of these murderers. The miners must have protection.' These points were made in their pressure for a quick meeting. So it was that Mike Kilner was elected sheriff, without opposition as there was no other candidate.

When the meeting broke up Naylor took Kilner to his room. He offered the new sheriff a cheroot and when both men were settled on their chairs Naylor looked shrewdly at Kilner.

'I'm mighty pleased you were elected, Mike,' said Naylor. 'You should have had the job before, but I figure it was only a matter of time before you got it. I reckon you and I can work close together for the good of the town.'

Mike Kilner waited a moment before speaking as if he were seeking the right approach. 'I think we'd better put all our cards on the table,' he said, coming straight to the point. 'You wanted me in because you thought I could be bought; you want to rule this town, you want things your way so you can make a fortune. No doubt you checked on my past, well, I've done my own checking on your methods.' He saw the surprise in

Naylor's face. 'Don't look alarmed,' he went on. 'I'll play along for my cut, but I thought you'd better know right from the start that I'm no fool and that we know where we stand.'

Naylor laughed loudly and pushed himself from his chair. 'Well, I can see you and I are going to hit it off. This calls for a drink.' He crossed the room to a large oak sideboard and poured out two whiskies. Whilst they drank he outlined his immediate plans to Mike Kilner.

The next day those plans were being put into operation, for when Jed arrived at the camp in Blackfoot Canyon he found the new sheriff already there, talking to the miners, absolving the Masters stage-line from any guilt or neglect and putting forward new plans to cope with the robbers.

Jed thanked Mike for his support but asked him why he was making his plans public knowledge. 'The gang are sure to get to know them.'

'If they know I'm going to place men along that hillside they won't be able to pull that boulder trick again,' pointed out the sheriff.

Jed agreed but was suspicious of the idea. However, Kilner's theory proved correct.

The next time the stage was due to go through with gold the gang tried to get into the same positions as before but they were driven off by Sheriff Kilner's men. This resulted in the following stage shipping gold being attacked in more open country and Jed's patrol was able to keep them away. Each time the sheriff came in for praise and people lost no time in saying that if he had been elected in the first place none of the robberies would have occurred. But Jed had his suspicions; things seemed to have gone too smoothly too suddenly.

Following the safe arrival in Boulder of this second shipment of gold Jed voiced his opinion to his brother.

'I'm convinced these last two raids were put-up jobs to make the sheriff look good.'

'Just what I thought,' exclaimed Clance. 'The attacks weren't really pressed.'

'You realise what that could mean?' asked Jed.

'Sure. Mike Kilner's working in with this gang but it will take some proving. Besides look how popular he's gettin'. Say anythin' against him an' no one will listen. But what I don't understand is, if the idea is to get the gold, why a sham attack?'

'I think it goes deeper than Kilner and this

121

gang. I believe Bart Naylor's behind this,' replied Jed. He paused and Clance let out a whistle.

'You're probably right an' I'll go along with you on that but that's goin' to take more provin' than Kilner's shady side.'

'I know,' replied Jed, 'but we've got to work on it otherwise Naylor will get such a grip on this town that he'll be running it and we'll be forced out.'

'But things were really goin' against us,' pointed out Clance. 'If he was behind those hold-ups why this sudden switch. Confidence in us was at a low ebb but not now.'

'This is how I see it,' explained Jed. 'We turned down a bid by Naylor. This, coupled with the fact that I out-smarted him in his attempt to get Dave Harman's strike, annoyed him. He was determined to get even with me and at the same time force us into a position where we would have to sell. This I think he would have done through hold-ups and so getting the stage-line a bad name with resultant loss of trade.'

'That's exactly what was happening, so why the change?' put in Clance.

'That's the way he wanted it to happen if Mike Kilner had been elected sheriff the first time; something would have been worked to show Kilner wasn't to blame. But, when Walt Cooper was elected sheriff, Naylor had to think again when the attempt to kill him that first night failed. He couldn't try another murder attempt so the stage robberies were made to serve another purpose, that of getting rid of Cooper. This he succeeded in doing but of course people's trust in the law was now weak, he had to build it up again because he needs a sheriff in his hands whom people will trust, that's why these recent raids have been made to fail.'

'All right, but at the same time he's not forcin' us out,' pointed out Clance.

'Maybe not, but if I'm right so far in my theorising, and I reckon I'm not far off the truth, Naylor will try to hit us some other way, so we've got to be on our guard.'

'Could we get at him through this gang?' queried Clance.

'It's a possibility,' agreed Jed. 'Even if it doesn't help us to prove it openly it could give us a lead. If we knew who was leading this gang we would know if there was any association with Naylor and maybe with Kilner.'

'Right,' said Clance, 'then I propose to do a bit of trailin'. We'll make some excuse for me not to ride with the next shipment. I'll follow. If it is attacked, I'll try to follow the gang.'

Jed agreed to the idea and the plan was discussed in detail.

It was three days later before they were able to implement their ideas. The stage was carrying a large consignment of gold and nothing was done to disguise the fact.

'Everything ready, boys?' asked Sheriff Kilner as he joined Jed and Clance beside the coach.

'Yes,' replied Jed, 'but there's been a slight change in our set-up.' The sheriff looked surprised, he did not want alterations. 'Mel Lockhart's going to drive the stage, I'm taking Clance's place with the patrol.'

'Oh, is that all,' said the sheriff. He was relieved that there was no serious change in the plans. 'What's the matter with Clance?'

'I want him to stay here, I've been told that some of the miners up the far reaches of the canyon might be coming in with some gold.'

The sheriff nodded. 'Right, then let's roll.'

Clance watched the stage and its outriders leave the camp. There was always a crowd on such an occasion and Clance decided to wait until it had dispersed before he left. He made his departure inconspicuous but once out of sight of the camp he put his horse into a gallop to close the distance between himself and the stage. Once he had it in his sight he checked his speed and proceeded cautiously so that none of the protection riders would see him.

They passed the site of the boulder attacks and then moved into a wider valley. Everything was going smoothly. Clance decided to leave the trail and made for a small knoll about a quarter of a mile away. He figured it would give him an advantageous view of the stage as it proceeded along the valley. He left his horse at the bottom of the rise and scrambled quickly to the top, lying flat on his stomach so as not to be conspicuous. Clance had only just settled himself into position when there was an outburst of gunfire.

Several men broke from cover to the left of the stage, but Clance saw that they had timed their appearance just that shade too late. The coach was already moving at full gallop, Mel had not lost a moment in seizing the opportunity of a clear trail ahead. The raiders turned in pursuit but once they met the opposition of the protection riders they broke off the attack. It was all over very quickly. To all outward appearances the strength of the escort men was too much for the hold-up men but to Clance, studying the whole affair from a distance, it looked a put-up job, very skillfully executed and really only obvious to anyone looking for such an attempt.

As the attackers broke away to the left of the trail Clance scrambled quickly to his feet and ran back to his horse. He leapt into the saddle and rode quickly to the trail where he paused just long enough to check on the riders' direction. They were still moving up the hillside and Clance started to move at a tangent to their track in order to be close to them when he came behind them. As the angle between himself and the riders began to narrow he had to proceed more cautiously for he dare not risk being seen. Even so he was almost caught unawares when the group of horsemen suddenly swung left at right angles to their track, moving in a direction which would bring them close to Clance. He just had time to pull his horse round behind a group of boulders. He slid from the saddle quickly and held his horse by the bridle soothing it with softly spoken words. One slight sound and all would be lost. His nerves were tense as he listened to the sound of the pounding hooves coming nearer and nearer. The gang passed barely fifty yards away but so intent were they on their ride that not one glanced in Clance's direction. Clance almost whooped for joy when he saw them. He recognised four men whom he had seen around Boulder and there was no mistaking their leader, Carl Frome. Frome had been linked with Bart Naylor in Denver and Jed had named him in backing up Naylor's attempt to get on one of the first stages to leave Denver.

He let the riders get some distance ahead before he climbed into the saddle and put his horse into cautious pursuit. The gang kept moving, parallel to the trail and after about three miles the going became rougher and the hillside was strewn with boulders, making Clance's task easier. Suddenly the riders dropped from Clance's sight and a few moments later he found himself staring down into a hollow in the hillside in which there was evidence of a camp. From his cover Clance watched the men swing from their saddles. They were laughing and joking and seemed far from upset that their attempt to get the gold had been futile. Clance felt more convinced than ever that Jed's theories must be correct. Soon they would be tested further when Clance reported the whereabouts of the gang's hide-out. He hurried back to his horse, led it quietly for some distance before mounting and heading with all possible speed for Boulder.

8

When Clance reached Boulder he found that the stagecoach had not been in long and there were still plenty of people hanging around the office discussing the attack. Wanting to have a word with his brother first, Clance made his way to the rear of the office and when he entered by the back door he was pleased to find only Jed and Mel there.

'Clance!' gasped Jed. 'Why the back way? Something wrong?'

'No,' replied Clance. 'Just didn't want to attract attention an' wanted you to have the news first.' Jed nodded and eagerly waited for his brother to continue. 'The robbers were led by Carl Frome,' announced Clance.

'Frome!' gasped Jed. 'We might have guessed.'

'This looks like a tie-in,' said Mel.

'Sure does,' agreed Jed, 'but we'll need

proof. Do you know where they're hiding, Clance?'

'Yes, followed them to a small hollow,' replied his brother.

'Good. Then let's go and see the sheriff. He'll have to form a posse to go after them. Maybe Frome will talk,' said Jed.

'There are plenty of us to go after them if we get Red and the others,' suggested Clance.

'We've got to keep it legal,' said Jed. 'Besides, Red and the others are getting ready to leave for Denver, some big orders have come in during the last couple of days and the goods have got to be brought. In any case I want to see Mike Kilner's reactions.'

Jed and Clance hurried to the sheriff's office only to find he was not there. They crossed to the *Golden Nugget* and found Kilner at the bar talking to Bart Naylor. Bart greeted them amicably, calling for two more beers.

'Thanks,' said Jed, 'but we'll have to forget the beers, there's some riding to be done, sheriff. Clance knows where the robbers are hiding.'

'What!' The information drew surprise from both Kilner and Naylor and for just a moment Jed thought he detected alarm in the sheriff's eyes. Naylor on the other hand gave nothing away.

'That's good work,' said Kilner, 'but I thought you were supposed to be staying in Blackfoot Canyon.'

'That's the story we gave out,' replied Clance, 'but the real purpose was so that I could trail anyone who attacked the stage. If I had been in the patrol I would have been under orders to stay with the coach.'

'Right,' agreed the sheriff.

'That was smart thinking,' congratulated Naylor. 'Your idea or your brother's?'

Clance ignored the question and went on quickly to tell them how he had followed the gang. When he had finished his story Kilner could do nothing else but call a posse. Half an hour later, twenty men, including Jed and Clance, were on their way out of Boulder.

Two miles from the hollow Clance turned off the trail. The pace became slower over the rougher ground and Clance slowed it even further about half a mile from the hollow so that the gang would not be warned of their approach by the noise of the horses. A quarter of a mile from their objective, Clance pulled to a halt.

'We'd better go on foot from here,' he whispered.

The sheriff nodded and signalled the men to dismount. They drew their rifles from the scabbards and after Kilner had designated a man to look after the horses, they moved away in the direction of the hollow. As they neared it the sheriff signalled to the men to spread out. A few yards from the edge of the hollow they dropped to their stomachs and crept forward cautiously. Astonishment seized them when they looked into the hollow.

'What's this, Masters, are you foolin' with me?' bellowed the sheriff, rising to his feet.

'This is where I saw them,' shouted Clance. 'I'm not havin' you on. They were here, I saw them, led by Carl Frome.'

'Well, they aren't here now,' sneered Kilner disbelievingly as he started down the slope.

The men examined the hollow and it was evident that it had been used as a camp by several men. The sheriff, although he proclaimed they only had the evidence of one man, was forced by pressure from the other riders to scout the area. Their efforts to find some other proof to substantiate Clance's story proved fruitless. The gang had hidden their tracks well when they had moved.

When the posse returned to Boulder, Jed

and Clance went straight to their office where Mel Lockhart informed them that Red, with his wagon crew, had left for Denver and Vance Wells had brought a full complement of passengers in on the stage from Denver. Jed told Mel of their wasted efforts to catch the robbers.

'It looks as if they were tipped off,' commented Mel.

'Nothin' more certain,' agreed Clance.

'I would say that the sheriff is definitely connected,' said Jed thoughtfully. 'That posse could have been away from Boulder sooner than it was – delaying tactics by Kilner to give the gang time to be warned.'

'Considerin' the rumoured connections between Frome and Naylor and the keenness of Naylor to get Kilner into office, I figure they're all connected.'

'I reckon you're nearer the mark,' agreed Jed, 'but as we can't prove anything, we'll have to play a waiting game and keep our eyes and ears open.'

Bart Naylor had watched the return of the posse from the window of the *Golden Nugget*. He had been relieved to find them return empty-handed. The man whom he had sent off from Boulder to warn Frome and tell him to go to the hide-out at Slim Butte had certainly made good use of the time given to him by the delay in the posse leaving town engineered by the sheriff. Naylor smiled to himself as he turned away from the window. Things were going his way nicely, he had certain of the leading citizens playing along with him; the sheriff was an instrument in his hands, he had clamped down on gambling in the tent city, thus forcing the miners to frequent the *Golden Nugget* where his gambling tables were reaping a rich reward; and two large gold consignments from the stage were his. The only people really troubling him were the Masters brothers; if they were not dealt with they could upset things, especially after Clance Masters had trailed Carl Frome. Property and businesses were coming into Naylor's hands and if only he could gain control of the biggest and most influential concern in Boulder – the Masters Overland Stage – then either directly or indirectly he would control the town and, moulding it for his own ends, would become a very rich man.

He strolled to the bar where the barman poured him a whisky, which he sipped thoughtfully, waiting for the sheriff to come and make his report.

Naylor realised that by discrediting the stage-line in the eyes of the miners he could probably force it out of business and this he had set out to do, but Jed Masters always seemed to be that one step ahead of him. With the election of Walt Cooper as sheriff Naylor had used the attacks on the stage to get rid of him. When Mike Kilner was made sheriff confidence in the post of lawman had to be re-established and so Naylor had faked the raids on the stage, but this had also had the effect of restoring trust in the Masters stage-line. Now Naylor realised he must get at Masters some other way.

The sheriff arrived a few minutes later, and under the pretence of a friendly drink he informed Naylor about the patrol of the posse.

'We are going to have to watch those two brothers and their outfit carefully,' pointed out Naylor, 'and it is virtually useless to carry on the attacks on the stage.'

'Then how are you goin' to git at them?' asked Kilner.

'I've been making plans,' replied Naylor lazily. 'I'm going up to Slim Butte to see Frome tomorrow, you keep an eye on things and especially on those two brothers.'

The following morning Jed was in the

office with some paper work when Clance hurried in.

'I took my horse to the blacksmith's and on my way back here I saw Bart Naylor ridin' out of town,' said Clance. 'Struck me he might be worth following.'

'He might at that,' agreed Jed. 'Not very often he's seen on horseback.' He pushed himself to his feet. 'I'll trail him, you'd better delay leaving for Blackfoot Canyon.'

Jed grabbed his Stetson and a few minutes later he was taking the north trail out of Boulder in pursuit of Naylor unaware that his own activities had attracted the curiosity of the sheriff.

Naylor kept to a steady pace, there was no need for undue haste and the day was hot. Jed was curious as to why he was heading in that direction, the north trail was little used, it was rough and led into the high country. He could not even hazard a guess as to Naylor's destination for there were several side trails forking into the rough terrain. When the sheriff realised that Jed was trailing Naylor he began to think of ways of stopping him.

His mind toyed with the problem. He knew Naylor did not want any cold-blooded murder that could be investigated, and no doubt the killing of Jed Masters would stir up a hornets' nest. An 'accident' such as happened to Walt Cooper was another matter, but try as he could Kilner could think of no way of faking Jed's death. He came to the conclusion that the best thing would be to try to scare Jed off before Naylor's destination became apparent.

Accordingly he held back until the trail led through a landscape of rock protrusions. By skilful use of cuttings in the great outcrops of rock, and judicious use of massive boulders as cover the sheriff was able to move up the hillside to the right and outride Jed. Kilner halted his horse and after securing it took his rifle from its leather scabbard and slipped to an advantageous position overlooking the trail amongst a group of boulders on the edge of a fifty-foot drop. He overlooked the trail where it came out of a cutting. Kilner positioned himself comfortably with his rifle resting between two boulders. He found himself going tense as the moments passed, then suddenly Jed was there, moving slowly on his horse. Kilner took aim, he was cool, calm, all the tension had gone from him. He squeezed the trigger slowly. The crash of the rifle reverberated amongst the rocks and Kilner saw Jed, startled by the unexpected, turn his horse sharply and gallop back into the cutting.

Jed was swinging out of the saddle as he reached cover. He dropped to the ground and jerked his Colt from its holster as he fell behind a boulder. He crouched there for a few moments expecting another shot, but none came. His brain was racing. The bullet had been unpleasantly close and Jed wondered who had tried to kill him. Could Naylor have tumbled to him and doubled back to lie in wait? Jed was determined to find out. He peered cautiously round the boulder. No shot came. Jed was puzzled. Had the would-be assassin cleared off after one shot which, it must have been obvious, had not hit Jed? The pound of hooves drew his attention and, with his gun ready, he waited for the rider to make his appearance.

Suddenly Bart Naylor appeared at full gallop and almost in the same instant he spotted Jed. He hauled on the reins, bringing his horse to a sliding halt. Naylor glanced round anxiously.

'What's wrong?' he shouted, struggling to steady his horse.

'Someone took a shot at me,' yelled Jed.

Naylor dropped from the saddle and crouched beside Jed. Jed realised his theory about Naylor was wrong; he could not possibly have fired the shot and got down to the trail to be here now.

'Any idea who it was?' asked Bart.

'No,' replied Jed. 'I didn't see him. Funny thing is he only fired once even though he must have known he missed me.'

'Maybe he's gone,' said Naylor.

'I figure the shot came from behind those rocks on top of that sheer drop,' said Jed.

Naylor peered round the boulder, studied the situation for a moment, then said, 'Right, Masters, I'll take the left-hand side, you take the right-hand; we'll circle him.'

Jed nodded and both men crept away. Jed's thoughts were on Naylor as he moved up the hillside. Surely he couldn't have arranged this otherwise he would not have been prepared to offer assistance so readily, besides he couldn't have been certain Jed would follow him. Jed was puzzled. Naylor was equally puzzled. It was obvious that Masters was trailing him; had Kilner trailed Masters and tried to kill him? Naylor cursed him for a fool if he had and he only hoped that if it was Kilner he was not hanging about.

Both men reached the group of rocks together. Their caution was completely unnecessary for they found no one there.

'Wal, looks as if he's flown,' said Naylor, slipping his Colt back into its holster.

'Yes,' agreed Jed disappointedly. Both men started to make their way down the hillside. 'You ride this way often?' asked Jed.

'Occasionally,' replied Bart. 'I like it up here, but if people are going to get shot at … well…' He paused and looked at Jed with a smile. 'Don't tell me it's one of your favourite rides.'

'No,' replied Jed. 'I was wondering if there was any possibility of using it as a stage-route, we could cut out a few miles of the ride to Blackfoot Canyon.' He knew this was a lame excuse and that it was unlikely that Naylor would believe him.

'Stage route?' said Naylor in amazement. 'Too rough for that, I thought you would have known.'

Both men were fencing with words and realised the other was trying to cover up the real reason for riding the north trail. The shot had betrayed Jed's presence. Naylor knew Jed could not continue to follow him and Jed realised it would be useless to do so.

'I guess you're right about it being too rough, I'm wasting my time up here, I may as well return to Boulder,' said Jed.

'Guess so,' agreed Naylor.

Jed collected his horse, swung into the saddle and with a nod to Naylor, reluctantly turned his horse in the direction of Boulder. He was tempted to resume the trailing of Naylor but he knew it would only lead him into deeper trouble.

Bart Naylor watched Jed ride away and, after he had passed from sight, Bart climbed on to his horse and followed. When he was satisfied that Jed was keeping on the trail to Boulder and making no attempt to resume his shadowing, Naylor turned his horse and retraced his steps.

About half a mile beyond the place where he had encountered Jed, Bart rounded a bend in the trail to find Mike Kilner relaxing in the saddle smoking a cheroot. Naylor nodded a greeting as he halted beside the sheriff.

'Did you fire that shot at Masters?' he asked.

'Yes,' answered Kilner with a smile. 'I figured to scare him off when I knew he was trailin' you. A killin' would have been hard to explain away satisfactorily.'

'Good work,' praised Naylor. 'It worked a treat, once he knew that I knew he was there and that someone else was watching him he had to call it off. He's heading back to

Boulder now. Reckon you'd better get back there as well.'

The two men discussed the situation for a few moments before parting. An hour later Bart Naylor was leading his horse through a narrow cutting in the rock-face near Slim Butte. The narrow passage gave into a small hollow completely surrounded by walls of rock. It was a perfect hide-out. He was glad he had taken the precaution of advising Carl Frome to find a hiding place in case it was wanted and then, with the usual Naylor thoroughness, had taken a look at it himself. He was greeted amiably by Frome's gang. Taking Frome to one side he warned him.

'You'll have to watch your step with the Masters brothers. You were careless not to check for followers. You were seen and recognised. It was a good job they called the sheriff in to form a posse and didn't take it into their own hands, as it gave me time to warn you.'

'I'm sorry, boss,' apologised Frome, knowing he had got a little too confident.

'All right, forget it, but be careful in future. Jed Masters followed me today, so they must think there could be a connection between us. We've got to move in on them fast.'

'Do you want us to press home the attacks

on the stage?' asked Frome.

'No, we'll have to forget that,' replied Naylor. 'We'll hit them where it will hurt more, their freighting business.'

When Bart Naylor set out on the return journey to Boulder he left behind a man in full possession of a plan aimed at the end of the Masters Overland Stage.

The following day Carl Frome sent two of his men to a vantage point overlooking the trail between Denver and Boulder with strict instructions that, as soon as they sighted Masters's freight wagons on their way to Boulder, they were to return with the news immediately.

Two days later the two men left their look-out posts and headed back into the high country with the information required by Carl Frome. That same night Frome led his gang under cover of darkness at a steady, purposeful pace to Boulder.

9

The day on which the freight wagons arrived in Boulder proved to be one of the rare occasions when all the men employed by the Masters Overland Stage were in town together. Vance Wells had had a quiet run with the stage from Denver, Clance Masters had accompanied Mel Lockhart on the stage from Blackfoot Canyon and about mid-afternoon Red, Tay, Sam and Buck had brought the freight wagons in. The demand for goods had been so great that Red had used his own initiative and purchased, in Jed Masters's name, a third wagon in Denver. They had been laden to overflowing but Red and his crew had brought them to Boulder without mishap. The unloading of the wagons into the big wooden building, which Jed had purchased when he saw the necessity of a storage depot with the expansion of the freighting business, had taken place immediately.

When he was satisfied that all was in order, that the wagons and stagecoaches were parked alongside the store and the horses were comfortable in the stable attached to the building, Jed told his men to meet him in the *Golden Nugget* after they had cleaned up.

They were enjoying the relaxation after the hard work. Jed was feeling particularly satisfied with the way things were going. Business was booming and he could see only expansion ahead. He had around him young men who were interested in the business, men who were prepared to use their own initiative, men whom he could trust and whom he felt would do anything for him. He had shown his appreciation by adding a bonus to their wages and now the beer was flowing freely.

It was close on ten o'clock when two men burst into the *Golden Nugget*. Their shouts of 'Fire!' pierced the rowdy noise of the saloon and brought a momentary, incredulous silence. In that brief moment, before pandemonium broke out and there was a rush for the street, Jed and his men caught the words 'the stage-line's store'. They looked at each other in horrified, disbelieving amazement and then they were racing for the doorway. As they burst from the saloon they saw a glow in the sky from the direction of the store.

Jed, with his men close on his heels, raced across the roadway towards the side street which led to the store. As they rounded the corner chill gripped Jed when he saw flames leaping up the walls of the building. People seemed to be coming from all sides and when they reached the end of the street they found that two chains of water-buckets had been formed.

Jed sized up the situation in a flash and issued orders quickly and decisively. 'Red, Tay, the horses.' The panting men raced off again. 'Sam, Buck, get some helpers and move the wagons.' The two men found willing helpers around them and hurried off. 'Clance, let's see if we can save anything.'

The two brothers ran towards the main door followed by a group of men willing to do what they could. One of the bucket-chains was throwing the water at the door up which a mass of flames were leaping, but Jed soon saw their efforts would be no use. The fire had too great a hold on the double doors.

'Round to the side door,' yelled Jed. 'Maybe we can push them open from the inside.'

The front wall was a mass of flames but once they were round the corner Jed saw that the fire had not such a hold on the side wall and that there was a chance for them. Jed soon had the door unlocked and they burst into the building. Two walls were a roaring inferno and it would not be long before the whole building was a mass of flames.

Jed yelled to Clance and they grabbed a long pole which was lying beside the wall. Holding the pole in front of them they moved towards the flaming door. They pushed at it, but the flames forced them back. They tried again but the lock on the door held firm. There was a sudden roar on their right as part of the wall crashed in; sparks flew everywhere and when Jed glanced round he saw that some of the goods were already on fire and the efforts of the other men to beat them out were proving of no avail. In the same glance he saw that the devouring flames had more than a firm grip on the building. He realized that even if they succeeded in getting the door open there would be little chance of saving anything; besides, men's lives would be endangered in the attempt for the roof and beams were being eaten at by the fire.

'Everyone out,' yelled Jed above the roar. He and Clance dropped the pole and signalled to the men to leave the blazing building. They reached the door and, as they started to file out, another section of the wall crashed in. Once they were outside Jed signalled to everyone to move away from the blazing building. He was thankful that the building stood on its own and, as far as he could see, no other erection was in danger. He warned the men who had been using the buckets to keep them filled and keep a look-out in case any sparks did reach the nearest building.

Sam and Tay came running up the street and sought out Jed and Clance.

'We've got the wagons and coaches pushed out of the way on to the main street,' panted Sam.

'Good work,' praised Jed, 'but after this loss I can't see us wanting them,' he added despondently. 'Wonder if Red and Tay managed to save the horses.' The complete building was a burning mass and Jed knew if his men had not saved the horses they would be unable to do so now. He started off towards the stable.

When Red and Tay reached the stable they were thankful to find the situation was not impossible. One wall was on fire and the two men realised that they would have to work quickly if they were to save nearly thirty horses. They pushed at the door and flung it open to be met with a great outpouring of billowing smoke. The two men staggered back away from the choking thickness and pulled their neckerchiefs over their mouths and noses. With its release the smoke thinned inside the stable. As Red and Tay ran forward the frightened cries and stamping hooves of the horses pounded in their ears.

The horses were tugging at the ropes holding them in their stalls and, with smoke pouring around them, the two men realised it would be courting disaster to try to squeeze past each frightened horse to cut it loose. Red glanced around desperately, seeking some way to save the animals. The wall behind them was blazing furiously and the flames were beginning to get a grip on the rafters and roof.

Red pulled down his neckerchief and put his mouth close to Tay's ear.

'Got your knife?' he shouted above the noise. 'We'll have to work our way along the hay racks at the back of the stalls.'

Tay nodded and ran to one end of the stable, shielding his face against the heat from the flames. Red pulled his neckerchief back across his face, took his knife and ran to the opposite end of the stable. He climbed on to the wooden partition between the two stalls and inched his way as quickly as possible to the wall. On either side of him the horses jerked at their retaining ropes. Reaching the wall Red swung down on to the hay rack in the first stall and with one swift stroke of his knife severed the rope. Suddenly finding itself free the horse stamped backwards out of the stall, but, as it turned, its fear was intensified by the sight of the flames. It twisted, wondering which way to go to escape the terror. It made as if to come back into the stall, but, immediately he saw this, Red dropped to the ground waved his arms and yelled at the top of his voice. The animal turned back and moved away from the stall. Sensing freedom and escape it moved towards the door. When a horse came from the opposite direction and turned towards the door it followed.

Red did not waste a moment once he saw the horse move away from the stall. He climbed back on to the hay rack and clambered over the partition to the next stall where he slashed the rope. The horse moved backwards, and, although frightened by the roaring flames, followed its companions to safety. Red worked as swiftly as he could, all the time keeping an eye on the movement of the flames.

Suddenly there was a great crash from the end of the stable as one of the rafters fell in and showered sparks everywhere. Red was concerned for Tay but he kept up his freeing of the horses, hoping as he neared the middle stall to see Tay. Red severed the rope in the middle stall realising that he had already over-stayed the safety margin, but he could not bring himself to leave any of the horses to be burned alive. He clambered into the next stall, released the frightened horse and started to climb into the next stall. He suddenly realized it was empty. Where was Tay? He felt sure Tay felt as he did about horses and would not have left one whilst there was a chance to save it. 'Tay! Tay!' Red yelled at the top of his voice. Smoke swirled around him, flames leapt from the walls and rafters. Red dropped to the ground determined to search every stall for Tay. As he moved out of the stall he fell over something and as he turned he realised it was Tay. Red grasped him with his powerful hands and dragged him upwards. At the same he bent forward so that Tay fell across his right shoulder. Red straightened and grasping Tay round the legs, he staggered out of the blazing building, coughing and almost choking with the smoke. Once free of the fumes he gulped air into his aching, smarting lungs. His eyes, streaming with water, made out forms rushing towards him, then he felt strong eager hands, helping him, relieving him of Tay. He heard the familiar voice of his boss. 'Good work, Red, you'll be all right.' Then everything went black and he pitched into oblivion.

When Red appeared from the stable carrying Tay, Jed yelled for someone to get the doctor and led the rush to help his men. Tay was taken out of Red's arms and laid gently on the ground at a safe distance from the burning building. When Red collapsed he was laid beside Tay and a few moments later the doctor was kneeling beside them giving them the best of his attention. Jed, Clance and the other men of Masters Overland Stage stood by, anxiously awaiting his verdict. Relief swept over them when the doctor reported that they would be all right.

'Give them plenty of air, they'll soon come round. Their burns are not serious. We'll get them to bed as soon as possible.'

Once they had seen to the needs of their two men, Jed and Clance turned their attention back to the blazing ruin of what had once been their store.

'There's nothing we can do about it,'

muttered Jed. 'It looks like the end of the line for us.'

'I wonder how that fire started,' mused Clance.

'Don't suppose we'll ever know,' replied Jed, 'but however it happened it's ruined us.'

Jed and Clance and most of the crowd hung around until they were sure no harm could come to any other building. As they walked slowly away from the smouldering ruins there were many sympathizers who offered their condolences. Jed and Clance returned to their office, and a few minutes later Vance, Mel, Sam and Buck filed in.

'We've seen to all the horses, boss,' said Vance. 'The livery stables are goin' to cope with them.'

'Thanks,' said Jed, but there was no enthusiasm in his voice.

'The horses, wagons and coaches are safe; can we continue to operate?' queried Sam.

'It's not as simple as that,' replied Jed. 'That was a big consignment that we lost tonight. It had been paid for by people asking us to freight it into Boulder for them. We've lost the goods so we'll have to refund those folks their money. I can't see the bank loaning me any more. I was expecting to start paying off some of the loan but now I won't be able to do that and in order to recompense the folks who have lost their goods I'll have to sell everything.'

'You'll give the bank a try first?' queried Vance.

'Sure, but I don't hold much hope,' replied Jed.

'We've got to keep goin',' said Vance.

A tap sounded at the door and the occupants of the office looked questioningly at each other. When Sam opened the door they were all surprised to see a small man who looked as though he had fallen on bad times look furtively right and left before stepping into the office. There was a frightened look in his wide eyes.

'Shut the door, quick,' he said irritably as Sam watched him walk into the room.

Sam automatically did as he was told and looked questioningly at Jed.

'Who's Jed Masters?' asked the newcomer in a high-pitched voice.

'I am,' said Jed, somewhat mystified.

'Who are these other fellas?' asked the stranger.

'This is my brother, Clance,' replied Jed, 'and these other men work for me.'

'Can I trust them?'

'I can,' replied Jed, annoyed at this question by a stranger, 'so I expect you can. Now what do you want?'

'Don't be snappy,' returned the stranger, regaining some measure of confidence when he realised he had nothing to be afraid of from these men.

'You looked scared when you came in here, somethin' troublin' you?' asked Clance.

'I was. Didn't want anyone seein' me come here,' answered the small man. 'I was cuttin' down past your warehouse tonight just before the fire started.' He paused and glanced anxiously at the faces around him. All were eagerly awaiting what would follow this announcement.

'Go on,' prompted Jed. 'Did you see anything?'

'Two men hurryin' away from the building! They almost bumped into me.'

'Did you recognize them?' asked Jed eagerly.

'No. Hardly got a look at them.'

'Would you recognize them again?'

'Don't think so. It was dark an' they were on top of me an' away before I realized it. Didn't think much of it at the time but when the fire broke out I got to thinkin'.'

'Maybe the fire was deliberate!' put in Clance.

The man nodded. 'That's what I figured. I thought you would like to know, but then I got scared in case they'd got a good look at me, so I waited until now.'

'Anythin' else to tell us?' asked Clance.

The man shook his head. Clance pulled some dollars from his pocket and passed them to the man, who thanked him and turned to the door.

'What's your name?' asked Jed.

The man half turned. 'I'm not sayin', then nobody can get on to me,' he answered and shuffled to the door. He stepped outside quickly and was gone.

Everyone looked at Jed. 'So it was deliberate,' he hissed. 'Someone is really trying to put us out of business, and I'll guess who, but to prove it will be hard.'

'We've got to keep goin' somehow to give us time to get at Naylor,' pressed Mel.

'I don't see how,' replied Jed, 'but we'll fight as long as possible!'

10

Both Jed and Clance had a sleepless night, preoccupied as they were with the problems which faced them. They could find no answer to their predicament if the bank refused to advance them any more money, and, as they already had a big overdraft, they were under no illusions as to what the bank manager's answer would be.

A branch had been opened in Boulder but Jed and Clance rode to see the manager in Denver. He was sympathetic towards them, especially after hearing about the fire, but, as he explained, he could not let personal feelings rule the business of banking. The two brothers returned to Boulder faced with the prospect of selling their business.

'This is just what Bart Naylor wants,' said Jed. 'His grip on Boulder will be tighter than ever.'

'Must we sell to him?' asked Clance.

'He'll see no one else makes an offer,' answered Jed. 'It looks as though there's nothing else for it, but to see Naylor. May as well get it over now.'

They turned their horses towards the *Golden Nugget* where they slid from the saddles, hitched their horses to the rails and walked slowly inside.

'Naylor in?' Jed asked the barman.

'No, he's not in, but he shouldn't be long,' came the reply.

'May as well wait,' said Jed. 'Give us a couple of beers.'

The barman brought the drinks and the brothers sipped them in silence, each lost with his own thoughts. Ten minutes passed before they saw through the long mirror on the wall at the bar, Bart Naylor enter the saloon, look round and then come in their direction.

'Hello, boys,' greeted Naylor amiably. 'I was sorry to hear about your loss last night. Has it hit you hard?'

'I guess you know it has,' replied Jed testily.

'I'm not in the habit of prying into people's private affairs,' return Bart.

'You liar,' thought Jed. 'No doubt you arranged that fire and have been expecting us to contact you.' Instead he said, 'That fire has certainly altered things. I'm going to have to find some money from somewhere; those people whose goods we'd shipped from

Denver will have to be refunded.' Jed was not rushing to suggest a sale; he wanted to see Naylor's reactions. 'It certainly is a problem.'

'Have you tried the bank?' asked Naylor casually.

'We're already in debt to the bank and they won't advance any more,' replied Jed.

'Well, it looks as if you are in a jam,' commented Naylor. 'If you can't find the money I'd still be willing to buy your business; better still I'll make an offer now and if you like we can settle the deal right away.'

Jed rubbed his chin thoughtfully. 'You're rushing things a bit,' he commented with a wry smile. 'This needs talking over with my brother.'

'I don't see what else we can do but talk business with Naylor,' pointed out Clance. He did not see any sense in this parrying. They had no other solution to their predicament.

'Well, I guess so,' agreed Jed. 'Right, Naylor, we'll discuss terms.'

A smile of satisfaction spread across Naylor's face. At last he had got the Masters Overland Stage where he wanted it. With the exclusive right to run the passenger and freight traffic in and out of Boulder he could twist this town to his own ends.

'Give me a bottle of whisky, Joe,' he called to the barman. 'We'll have something to drink to, gentlemen.' He smiled at Jed and Clance. The barman handed him the bottle. 'Come along, we'll settle this matter in my office, come to an agreement and then I'll get my lawyer over from Denver to finalise everything.'

The three men started towards the door leading to the rooms at the rear of the building. They were half-way across the floor when the batwings burst open and a voice shouted.

'Jed! Jed Masters!'

The three men turned to see the bearded figure of Dave Harman hurrying across the room towards them.

Jed smiled when he saw the old miner, but his face became serious when he noticed the concern on Dave's face.

'Am I sure glad to find you,' said Dave as he reached Jed. 'I've just got into town, heard about your loss last night – I'm sure sorry. I reckoned you'd be hard hit so went to look you up in your office. Mel Lockhart told me you'd gone to Denver to try to raise some money but he'd seen you ride straight up to the *Golden Nugget* on your return. Did you get the money, son?'

'No, we didn't, Dave,' replied Jed. 'We're

just about to talk terms with Bart Naylor.'

'Sellin' him the business your father had faith in?' snorted Dave.

'I'm afraid it's as bad as that,' replied Jed.

'It's not,' said Dave firmly. 'I thought you'd be in a bad way, that's why I'm here. I've got plenty; you can have an indefinite loan with no strings attached.'

Jed and Clance stared in amazement at the old man. They could hardly believe their ears; this was something they had never dreamed about. They were speechless, shocked by the salvation offered to them.

'Wal, what do you say?' asked Dave, grinning at the expressions on their faces.

Jed suddenly let out a great whoop. A wide grin spread across his face and as he glanced at his brother he saw the eager expression giving approval to his acceptance.

'Thanks a lot, Dave, you don't know what this means to us,' he said, grasping the miner's hand. He turned to Bart Naylor whose face was clouding with anger at this sudden unexpected twist in the events.

'You promised me...' started Naylor, who felt his newly experienced power being snatched away from him.

'We promised you nothing,' cut in Jed excitedly. 'Only said we'd talk about it.'

Without waiting to hear what Bart said he swung round and grasped Dave by the arm. 'Come on, we'll talk this over in my office.'

Clance felt just as excited as his brother as he followed them out of the *Golden Nugget,* leaving behind an angry, fuming Bart Naylor swearing to get even with them before long.

Naylor watched the Masters Overland Stage revive from the severe blow it had taken and he eagerly awaited the chance for a revenge which would mean selling out to him. A week after the fire he received a surprise visit from his lawyer from Denver.

'What brings you here?' asked Naylor when the tall, square-faced man, with hair greying at the temples, entered his room at the back of the *Golden Nugget.*

'Two pieces of news I thought you would be interested in,' replied the lawyer, accepting a cheroot from the box held out by Naylor. 'Mind you,' he went, 'it is against all professional etiquette to divulge information.'

Naylor smiled. 'We've done business of this nature before, Curt, and you know I'm not ungrateful.'

'I just wanted to be sure we understood each other,' answered the lawyer smoothly. He paused to light his cheroot and Naylor waited anxiously for the information which he expected would help him to pull off another deal.

Curt blew a long cloud of smoke into the air. 'Well,' he said, 'the first piece of news is that old Dave Harman paid me a visit. Got me to make out his will.' He paused and drew at his cheroot. Naylor was puzzled; what did this have to do with him? He said nothing but waited for the lawyer to continue. 'He's made his will in favour of the Masters brothers, left everything to them!'

'What!' Naylor gasped at this surprise announcement. This certainly wasn't the type of information he had expected. His mind was racing with the significance of this news. No matter what he did to force the brothers to sell it would be of no avail. He could never financially embarrass them now for Dave Harman would continue to back them. Maybe they would sell out when Harman died but Naylor could not wait, he wanted the power now, besides he very much doubted if the brothers would give up the stage-line, there was a great deal of sentiment attached to it.

The lawyer had been watching Naylor and knowing Naylor's designs on the stage-line and Boulder he saw how hard this news had hit him.

'Maybe my next piece of news will soften the blow,' he said quietly. Naylor eyed him curiously. 'I've looked into the charter under which the Masters brothers operate. They have the exclusive right to operate the stage and freight lines between Denver, Boulder and Blackfoot Canyon, but there is one condition which says "unless convicted of a major crime".'

Naylor stared at the lawyer, his nimble brain already seeing solutions to his problems, linking the two pieces of information. If a murder could be planted on the two brothers then he could operate a stage-line without any complications but, if the victim was Dave Harman...!

'You've done well, Curt,' praised Naylor, excitement in his eyes.

'Thought you'd be interested,' smiled Curt. 'Could be a quick way to solve your difficulties.'

'Could be,' mused Naylor. 'I'll not forget this when things get sorted out.' He rose from his chair and poured out two glasses of whisky and both men drank to success.

The following day Bart Naylor rode to the hide-out near Slim Butte, being careful to make sure he was not followed. When he returned Carl Frome accompanied him and slipped quietly into the back of the *Golden Nugget* unseen.

Although Dave Harman protested against the decision, Jed and Clance insisted that he became a partner in the Masters Overland Stage. When they finally persuaded him that this was what they wanted and it would be better all round, seeing that he was putting money into the business, Dave informed them that 'it will be like keeping everything in the family, so to speak'. The boys had been puzzled but Dave had gone on. 'I've decided to take a trip to Denver and draw up my will and leave everything to you two.'

Jed and Clance had been speechless. They had protested. 'Haven't you got any relations?'

'No one. I came out west an orphan, an' I've got to leave my wealth to someone. I knew your father and have seen you grow up. I can think of no two people I'd rather leave it to. There is only one thing I ask you to do,' he had added. 'Keep the stage-line goin'.'

The brothers had made their promise and with an assured future for the business, Jed and Clance could not see Bart Naylor making any headway against them.

Four days after Carl Frome had ridden into Boulder with Bart Naylor, Naylor saw the opportunity he had been waiting for. All Jed Masters's men were out of town and when Dave Harman came into the *Golden Nugget* that evening Bart got into conversation with him and learned that Jed and Clance were also out of town but were expected back some time that night. This was just the sort of situation Naylor had been waiting for. When he left Dave, he set about putting his carefully thought out plan into operation.

A few minutes later the barman came up to Dave. 'I've just had a message from Jed Masters,' he said. 'He'd like to see you in the office in a few minutes if you would open up, he's just gone to see the sheriff.'

'Right,' said Dave. 'Sheriff? Did he say what was wrong?'

'No,' answered the barman and moved away to serve a customer.

Dave finished his drink and hurried out of the *Golden Nugget* He crossed the dark street, fumbled in his pocket for the keys to the office and let himself in. He was searching his pocket for a match when he heard the door open behind him. He half turned to greet Jed when a Colt crashed down on his head and he pitched to the

165

floor without a sound. He never felt the other blows which rained on his head.

Half an hour later Jed and Clance pulled to a halt outside their office. 'Funny there's no light,' commented Jed, as he swung from the saddle. 'I thought Dave would be waiting for us.' The two brothers stepped on to the sidewalk and Jed inserted his key into the lock. 'Strange,' he muttered, 'this door is unlocked.' He pushed the door open and they stepped inside. Clance scraped a match and in its flare Jed saw a huddled form on the floor. 'The lamp, quick,' he called. Clance lit the lamp and turned up the light.

Jed was on his knees beside the heap on the floor when Clance turned round.

'Dave!' gasped Clance. He shuddered when he saw the battered skull and realised there was no need to utter the question which had automatically sprung to his lips.

Jed's face was grim as he straightened. 'A brutal killing,' he muttered. 'Dave couldn't have had a chance. There wasn't even a struggle.'

'Why?' the question came from the tight lips of Clance. 'The safe hasn't been touched and there's nothin' of value here. Who'd want to attack a friendly old man like Dave?'

'I don't know,' whispered Jed thoughtfully.

'But I aim to find out. Was that lamp warm when you lit it?'

'No,' answered Clance.

'Then he must have been attacked just after he'd entered the office,' said Jed thoughtfully. 'He hadn't lit the lamp and it can't have been so very long ago, the blood's still wet. C'm on, we'd better get the sheriff.'

The brothers hurried out of the office and almost bumped into the sheriff who was strolling slowly along the sidewalk.

'You two boys in a hurry,' he remarked.

'Just coming for you,' replied Jed. 'Dave Harman's been murdered.'

'What!' The sheriff showed surprise and stepped past the two brothers into the office. He examined the body quickly, then asked Jed for his story. 'I wonder where Dave was before he came to the office?' he said when Jed had finished speaking.

'I guess the *Golden Nugget* wouldn't be a bad place to start,' suggested Clance.

'Good idea,' agreed the sheriff. 'I'd like you two boys along with me. Lock this place up.'

When the three men entered the *Golden Nugget* the sheriff made straight for the bar.

'Was Dave Harman in here tonight?' he asked the barman.

'Sure, left about half an hour ago after I

gave him your message, Mr Masters,' answered the barman.

'My message?' Jed stared incredulously at the barman. 'I didn't send him any message.'

The sheriff eyed Jed suspiciously and his hand moved a little nearer his holster.

'Sure you did,' said the barman. 'Fella came up to me an' said would I tell Dave Harman that you wanted to see him in the office right away.'

'Is that man still in the saloon?' asked Jed anxiously.

The barman looked round then shook his head. 'Nope,' he said crisply.

'Just as I thought,' muttered Jed.

'Did you send a message to Harman?' asked the sheriff.

'No,' snapped Jed. 'How could we? We've just got in to town.'

'The man mentioned your name,' put in the barman.

'You look to be in a tight jam,' said the sheriff.

'What do you mean by that?' asked Jed.

'I catch you hurryin' out of your office where there's the body of Dave Harman. You could have been tryin' to get away.'

'But we were comin' for you,' protested Clance.

'That's what you say,' returned the sheriff. 'Now I learn you sent for Dave.'

'We didn't,' stormed Jed.

'I've only your word for that,' answered the lawman. 'I'm placin' you both under arrest for the murder of Dave Harman pendin' further investigations.'

'What!' the brothers gasped incredulously.

Clance's hand moved to his Colt but Kilner outdrew him. 'I wouldn't try that,' he rasped.

A silence had gradually come on the *Golden Nugget* and the absence of noise brought Bart Naylor from his room. He showed surprise at the fact that the sheriff had his gun drawn on the Masters brothers and was in the act of disarming them. He smiled to himself as he stepped towards them. Things appeared to be going as he had planned.

'What's the trouble, Sheriff?' he asked.

'I'm arrestin' these two for the murder of Dave Harman,' replied Kilner.

'What?' Naylor feigned surprise. 'That's hard to believe. Why should they want to kill the man who had helped them?'

Clance seized on this. 'That's right; answer that one, Sheriff.'

'I don't know but I'm holdin' you both until I find out. Now move.' He motioned with his gun towards the door.

The brothers turned and walked slowly towards the door. As they walked down the street the *Golden Nugget* came to life again but now the atmosphere was charged with the conversation of murder. The sheriff locked them in adjoining cells but, as they were of the open bars type, they were able to speculate about their predicament after the sheriff had gone.

'I can't help feeling this is a big frame-up,' commented Jed.

'It must be,' answered Clance, 'but everythin' seems to fit so conveniently against us that it must have been carefully planned, but I can't see how plans could have been made so far ahead.'

Jed looked thoughtful. 'Maybe the plan was made and whoever it was waited for the right opportunity and that came tonight.'

'Then I plump for Naylor,' said Clance, 'particularly as the sheriff was mighty convenient to the office and was keen to arrest us.'

'Sure, he's in with Naylor,' agreed Jed. 'I only...' Jed stopped and let out a low whistle. 'I've got it. If we're convicted of murder we automatically lose the exclusive rights to the stage-line. I'd forgotten about that clause referring to a major crime.'

'Naylor must have found this out and engineered the whole affair,' gasped Clance.

'I reckon we've just about got it,' said Jed.

'The only thing is what about a motive for the killin'?'

'He'll soon provide a motive,' replied Jed.

11

Jed's words proved true all too soon. The town was seething with talk of the brutal killing and Bart Naylor made sure it kept that way until the next part of his plan was ready to unfold. Jed's men were concerned with the growing ugliness of the situation and after a long consultation with the two brothers they were briefed to keep their eyes and ears open for any clue as to the real killer.

Two days later a motive for the murder was produced when the lawyer from Denver arrived and announced that the Masters brothers were the sole beneficiaries under a will recently drawn up by Dave Harman. This was the right fuel for the fire of outraged anger which had permeated the whole town since the killing. With Carl Frome and his men circulating through the town the news soon got around and by the evening, with a continuous incitement against Jed and Clance, the town was in an ugly mood. The *Golden Nugget* was crowded and the talk was of practically nothing else but the murder and its outcome. Bart Naylor realised the situation just needed a little push and everything would go as planned. He had decided not to risk a trial, the brothers might be acquitted, after all the evidence against them was not conclusive.

Bart Naylor left the saloon and returned to his room where Mike Kilner and Carl Frome were waiting.

'The crowd out there look about ready,' said Naylor as he crossed the room. He chose a cheroot from the box on his desk and lit it thoughtfully. 'Kilner, you must put on a good show as the protecting sheriff; nobody must suspect that you give in easily. I know it can be dangerous for you, but I am a generous man.' The sheriff nodded without comment. 'Frome, you know what to do?'

'Sure,' grinned Frome. 'My men are in the saloon now. Once I start speakin' they'll go along with the idea, it won't take long to stir up a lynch mob, after our talk around town this afternoon.'

'Anyone say anything about the stage robberies and Clance Masters's identification of you?' asked Naylor.

'No,' answered Frome. 'Seems to have been forgotten in this new ruckus. At any rate an accusation wouldn't have held water with the predicament Clance Masters is in. Who'd take the word of a murderer?' Frome grinned. 'But I kept clear of the men working for Masters.'

'Good,' said Naylor. 'Well, I reckon you can go to work. See you both back here when it is all over.'

The two men left the room and whilst Frome went into the saloon Kilner made his way out of the back door and hurried to his office.

Whilst Carl Frome drank two glasses of beer he listened to the conversation around him and realised a few words'd easily turn these people into a howling, blood-thirsty mob. He called for a third beer and got into conversation with the group on his right.

'Well, I reckon the evidence is strong enough to condemn them,' one man was saying.

'Run right into the sheriff,' said Frome. 'A couple of moments earlier an' he would have caught them red-handed.'

'Well, I'd never have thought it of the Masters brothers,' said another man. 'They've been...'

'You never can tell what a man will do for money,' cut in Frome.

'Is it right then that Harman had made a will leaving them everything?'

'Sure is,' replied Carl, 'an' there's the motive, to get their hands on his fortune and mine as soon as possible.'

'Then they ought to be strung up!' said one of the group.

There was a murmur of approval from the rest. Frome seized his chance. 'They may get off if they're brought to trial.'

'It'll be a crime if they do.'

'Then why shouldn't we see they get the right verdict,' shouted Frome.

A roar of approval went up from the group of men which attracted the attention of others nearby. Frome played on their feelings, agitated subtlety, pronounced and denounced until the whole saloon was a seething mass of people with feelings running high against Jed and Clance. Suddenly a man jumped on to the bar.

'I say let's string 'em up now!' he yelled.

A yell of approval shook the room. Someone tried to protest but he was howled down.

'Then what are we waiting for?' shouted Frome. 'Let's go and get them.' He started to push his way towards the door and in a few moments the shouting, yelling crowd spilled out of the *Golden Nugget* on to the roadway. They spread out, filling the street, and set off for the sheriff's office. As if by magic two ropes appeared in someone's hands and flaming torches flared, adding a flickering eeriness to the grim scene.

Jed Masters's men were in the office discussing the situation when they were pitched into action by the appearance of the mob.

Vance was looking out of the window when the crowd suddenly burst out of the saloon. He gasped with horror when he saw them and realised their purpose.

'A lynch mob!' he shouted.

The other men were beside him in a flash.

'That's Carl Frome leading them,' said Mel.

'Then Bart Naylor must be behind it,' commented Red, 'and with a friendly sheriff things will sure go against Jed and Clance!'

'We've got to do something,' said Tay desperately.

Vance swung round from the window,

seeming to automatically take command. 'Come on,' he called. 'We need the horses, we can't stop that mob on foot.'

The men hurried out of the office by the back door which led into a small enclosure, three sides of which were occupied by stables. 'We'll need two spare horses,' called Vance. 'And make it snappy.' Sam had his saddled first and quickly saddled a second. Buck had also saddled two and as soon as they were ready the six men swung into the saddles and rode quickly out of the enclosure.

Vance led the way speedily along the back streets so that they would come on to the main street at the opposite side of the sheriff's office to the mob. Vance knew they would have to deal with the situation as it arose, but he figured they would be better off with more room in which to manoeuvre and he preferred to be facing the crowd rather than trying to control it from behind.

The sudden noise in the street brought both Jed and Clance to their feet. They exchanged horrified glances as the shouting seemed to take on a howl of some frenzied animal seeking a victim. The howl grew louder and louder.

'Mob!' whispered Clance, a terrible feeling gripping his stomach. 'They're comin' this way!'

Jed glanced at his brother and saw a certain terror in the eyes which stared widely and unbelievingly from a white face. 'Steady, Clance,' said Jed, trying to sound unworried. 'Sheriff!' he yelled. 'What's happening?'

The lawman came to the door leading to the cell block.

'Seems like someone's worked a mob up,' he said. 'But you needn't worry, they won't get in here.' He turned away but halted when Jed called out.

'Don't leave us in here, at least give us a chance if things go wrong.'

The sheriff grinned. 'What? And let you have a chance of jumpin' me and escapin'. Nothin' will go wrong.' He turned away, leaving the door open on purpose so that the two men would see into his office.

'What's he goin' to do against the mob?' commented Clance. He gripped the bars of the cell tighter until his knuckles showed white. 'Hi, sheriff, sheriff, let us out of here. We didn't kill anyone, you can't let them get us!'

'Clance!' shouted Jed. 'Get a hold of yourself; in that state you won't be able to take any chance which may crop up.'

Clance did not answer for a moment, then he looked at Jed. 'I'm sorry,' he muttered. 'It was that awful noise.'

'I know,' replied Jed. 'But be careful, something might turn up.'

The yelling and shouting had risen to a terrifying crescendo, then it began to quieten, and Jed and Clance knew that the sheriff, who had stepped outside, must be calling for order. They were anxious moments for the two men in the cells. They could hear Mike Kilner shouting but they could not make out his words. Someone in the crowd yelled and there was a great roar from the mob. There followed a confusion of shouts and sounds, a shot was fired, then suddenly the door of the office burst open and several men swarmed in pushing a disarmed sheriff before them.

'Carl Frome!' gasped Jed to himself when he saw the man in the lead. The lawman was pushed to one side and Jed guessed his had been only a token resistance. A man grabbed the keys from the desk and the men pushed into the cell block shouting and gesticulating at the men in the cells. The doors were unlocked quickly and Jed and Clance were dragged roughly from the cells, pushed through the office and forced outside.

As soon as they appeared a tremendous

yell went up from the mob. The two brothers shrank from what they saw. The light from the flickering torches betrayed the animal-like faces of the pack from which all reason had vanished. Nothing would stop this mob from violence. Jed and Clance struggled as powerful hands seized them and forced them down the steps on to the road. Cries of 'murderers', 'string 'em up', and all kinds of abuse were flung at them.

Carl Frome jumped down from the side-walk and stood arrogantly in front of the two men whose arms were being tied unceremoniously behind their backs. An evil grin of triumphant pleasure crossed his face.

'Soon you'll be no trouble to anyone,' he hissed.

'Meaning Naylor?' spat back Jed.

Frome did not answer, but Jed knew from the look that crossed his face that he was on the mark with his question.

'C'm on,' yelled Frome, 'let's get this over.' He turned and, with the mob yelling and shouting behind him, he led the way along the main street.

They had gone about thirty yards when six horsemen, with guns drawn, suddenly appeared out of a side street and strung themselves across the road facing the oncoming mob.

There was hesitation amongst the mob, and the shouting died to a murmur as men, faced with a turn in events which could possibly mean their own death, faltered. Carl Frome was taken aback by the appearance of the horsemen and, recognising Jed's riders, cursed himself for not having taken care of them first. He kept on walking, expecting the sheer weight of numbers to overcome the riders. They wouldn't dare shoot and possibly kill innocent townsfolk.

Jed and Clance exchanged hopeful glances and their hearts beat faster at the sight of their men and the possibility of escape.

Vance had held the men in the side street until he judged the moment was right to make their appearance. If they came on to the street too soon they would not form the great impression he wanted and too late would mean they would be too close. He saw a falter in the crowd, he heard the shouting subside and he saw Frome still keep coming forward and in that movement automatically draw the crowd after him. Vance fired two shots over the heads of the crowd.

'Hold it right there, Frome,' he yelled.

The crowd stopped, Frome hesitated then kept moving but this time he suddenly felt alone when he realised the mob no longer moved.

'Stay right there,' shouted Vance and loosed off a shot, spurting the dust at Frome's feet.

Frome stopped and glared angrily at Vance. Silence had descended on the crowd and they stared at the grim flame-lit faces of the riders, reading there a determination that would stand no nonsense. Although far outnumbering the riders, there wasn't one man in the crowd who would dare to draw his Colt, for each felt as if he was being watched.

'Release these two men,' ordered Vance.

There was reluctance amongst Frome's men who held Jed and Clance. Frome sensed this.

'You're breakin' the law helpin' two murderers to escape,' he shouted.

'You're takin' the law into your own hands,' called back Vance.

'They deserve it,' called Frome.

'Not without a trial and one that isn't worked up against them,' rapped Vance. 'Now free them.' There was a momentary hesitation until the six horsemen moved their horses forward menacingly a yard or two. Vance's Colt roared and the bullet whined close to Frome. 'The next one won't be a near miss,' shouted Vance. 'Now, let them go.'

Frome shuffled round and signalled reluctantly to his men. Feeling the hands release their grip, Jed and Clance ran forward. Mel bent down from the saddle and slashed their ropes quickly. A moment later Jed and Clance were mounted on the spare horses held by Sam and Buck. Vance and Mel held their position whilst the others turned their horses and rode into the side street. With their guns still menacing the crowd Vance and Mel backed their horses until they were opposite the same street. Vance yelled and both men pulled their horses round and were into the side street almost before the crowd realised it. Frome was prepared for the move and his Colt was out of its holster in a flash as soon as Vance and Mel turned, but his hasty shot was wide.

The eight horsemen put their animals into an earth-pounding gallop and were soon leaving Boulder. After a three-mile dead run Jed brought the group to a halt and they listened for any sound of pursuit, but there was no noise except the panting of their own horses.

Jed and Clance looked round their men. 'We sure owe you a lot. Thanks for all you've done. We'll never be out of your debt.'

Thanks flowed from their lips.

'What do we do now?' asked Clance.

'Well, I don't think we'll be followed,' said Jed. 'Frome and his cronies will realise its useless, by the time they get organised we could be anywhere in this darkness.'

'None of us is going to be able to return to Boulder,' pointed out Clance.

'Not at the moment,' agreed Jed. 'I can't see how we are going to prove our innocence, so we'll have to force Naylor's hand. Our first stop is Blackfoot Canyon.'

'What?' gasped Clance. 'With Dave Harman's murder hangin' over us the miners aren't goin' to be very friendly.'

'We've got to persuade them otherwise. I need their help.'

Jed said no more but turned his horse in the direction of Blackfoot Canyon.

12

Bart Naylor's immediate annoyance at the escape of the prisoners calmed when he studied the situation closely.

'Those brothers can't return to operate

the stage-line,' he commented to Mike Kilner and Carl Frome. 'I can take it over and start running it tomorrow. It is essential to Boulder and Blackfoot Canyon and I'm sure the Legislative will back me when I am doing a service. The Masters have branded themselves by this escape and there will be no one to support them. Kilner, you'll swear Frome and his gang in as deputies, then the Masters brothers and their riders can be hunted legally, besides I'm going to need the support of a strong and reliable law – there's sure to be some outbursts when the miners realize the grip I have on them.'

Kilner nodded. 'We'll do that right away if Frome will bring his men to my office.'

The two men made for the door but Naylor stopped them. 'Brief the new deputies to shoot to kill if ever they come across either of the Masters or any of their men. And have your men at the stage office at ten in the morning.'

Jed decided to lie low outside the camp at Blackfoot Canyon until the following morning. He discussed his plan with his men and, as day broke, they rode into the camp. They kept to their horses and it was not long before they were having to hold back miners, angry at the sight of the two supposed killers.

Jed held up his hands for silence as the men pressed around. 'Quiet,' he yelled. 'Give me a chance to explain what we are doing here.'

It was a few minutes before Jed got the silence he wanted. 'We didn't kill Dave Harman,' he called out. 'Things looked bad for us, but we didn't do it. Why should we?'

'Money,' yelled someone.

'Wanted the lot!' shouted another.

'What about the will?' called someone else.

'We knew about the will and maybe that gave us a motive if you look at it that way,' agreed Jed, 'but Dave Harman made us promise that when we came into his money we would still keep the stage-line running. Now he was already helping us to do that so there was no real benefit in killing Dave for his money.' He paused; there was some murmuring of agreement amongst the crowd. 'We were nearly lynched last night but thanks to my men we are here now. Carl Frome was leading that lynch mob – Carl Frome whom Clance identified as the leader of the gang who was robbing the stage of *your* gold. He was in town and that seems to prove to me that the sheriff is in with Carl

Frome, particularly as he did not press home the search for him. The sheriff was pushed into office by Bart Naylor and I believe all three are in this together. Naylor has a grip on Boulder which has been prevented from becoming too tight by our stage and freight line. No doubt now that we are out of the way he will attempt to take it over, getting the charter given to father altered because we are criminals and cannot run the line which is essential to Boulder. When he does that you can be sure he'll squeeze every dollar he can out of all of you.'

He paused to let his words sink in. He could see that the miners were impressed by his theories and when questions started flying at them both he and Clance answered them eagerly.

'Will you give us a chance and play along with us to smoke Naylor out?' he asked.

The miners agreed and Jed quickly explained his plan. 'First, I'm going to sell the stage-line to a group of you, at least on paper. We all ride to Boulder where you will lay claim to the business. From there on we will take things as they come from Naylor's reactions. It could be dangerous and there may be some gun play, but we'll all be on hand.' He went into the plan in more detail and a short while later Jed and Clance led a party consisting of their own six riders and six miners towards Boulder.

As they neared the town the party split up, the six miners riding openly into the main street whilst Jed led the others, after leaving Sam with the horses a short distance from the edge of the town, cautiously through the side streets to the stables and enclosure at the back of their office.

Tay kept watch in the side street and when he saw the miners cross the end of the street he signalled to the others. Buck, Red and Clance joined him and proceeded cautiously towards the main street, hiding behind some packing cases and barrels a short distance from the end of the street.

Jed, accompanied by Vance and Mel, moved carefully across the enclosure to the rear door of their office. Jed tested it cautiously and, finding it unlocked, pushed it slightly open. Voices came from inside.

'What's all this nonsense about?' snapped Bart Naylor irritably.

'My men are holding six miners at the door,' replied Carl Frome. 'They claim they own the stage-line.'

'What?' There was a note of derision in Naylor's voice. 'Ridiculous.'

'They claim Masters sold them the stage-line this morning an' that they have a document to prove it,' explained Frome.

The front door opened and the sheriff walked in.

'Glad you've got here, Kilner,' said Naylor irritation still in his tone. 'Get this nonsense sorted out. If there is a document and it looks legal, get your hands on it. Masters must have got to Blackfoot Canyon and he's trying to pull some stunt with these miners. I'm not having all my schemes upset now; Masters escaped all my attempts to ruin them, the murder frame slipped up when they escaped the lynching. They're on the run, so I don't want any fool spoiling things now.'

Jed heard the two men walk from the office, then drawing his Colt he pushed the door open. Naylor spun round and his eyes widened with astonishment when he saw Jed covering him with a gun.

'Thanks for the information,' said Jed quietly. 'I think you and your two cronies will be of interest to the law in Denver.'

There was a sudden commotion outside and a gunshot reverberated in the street. Jed's attention was deviated for a moment and Naylor seized on his chance. His Colt flashed into his hand and even as Jed fired

Naylor was squeezing the trigger. The bullet took Jed in the fleshy part of the arm whilst Naylor felt a pain across his left shoulder. He dived for the door and jerked it open to see Mike Kilner, smoking gun in hand, turning to face him, a look of astonishment, at the outburst of firing in the office, in his eyes. A bullet splintered the wood close to Naylor's head. He saw Frome's men, who had been on the sidewalk, diving for cover as three men appeared from the side street their guns blazing. The sheriff suddenly jerked as lead dug into his side. He staggered against the wall and fell, his hands clawing for support.

Naylor, terror in his eyes, realized he was caught. He turned, desperately seeking a line of escape. A miner lay on the sidewalk. One of Frome's men dived past him firing his Colt. Confusion seemed to reign everywhere as two sides faced each other in a gun battle. Only one man in the office between himself and escape seemed to be Naylor's best line. He flung himself back away from the whining bullets. His gun blazed but a look of astonishment crossed his face when he saw three men. Jed's bullet took him in the stomach. An incredulous look came into his eyes, and the gun slipped from a grip gone limp as his knees buckled and he pitched to the floor.

Vance and Mel leaped to the window. Somehow Frome had managed to slip to the horses tied to the rail. Shielded by the animal from the fire in the street he was untying one when he saw Vance appear at the window. His gun came up but Vance was quicker and Carl Frome pitched lifeless into the dusty road.

Realising that they were in a crossfire the rest of the gang threw down their guns and surrendered.

Cautiously Clance, Red and Tay, together with the miners, broke cover and came forward. Jed, Vance and Mel stepped from the office and when Clance saw that his brother was wounded he hurried to him.

'You all right?' he asked anxiously.

'Sure,' replied Jed with a grin, 'it's only a flesh wound. Red, Tay, take that lot and lock them up.'

As the two men escorted the prisoners to the sheriff's office, Jed turned to the miners. 'Thanks for all your help,' he said. 'Naylor was behind everything, Vance and Mel were witnesses to what he said and no doubt some of that gang will confirm it. I reckon we can run Masters Overland Stage for the benefit of Boulder and you miners now!'

The publishers hope that this book has given you enjoyable reading. Large Print Books are especially designed to be as easy to see and hold as possible. If you wish a complete list of our books please ask at your local library or write directly to:

Dales Large Print Books
Magna House, Long Preston,
Skipton, North Yorkshire.
BD23 4ND